OFF THESTICK

A VANCOUVER VIKINGS HOCKEY ROMANCE

SIERRA HILL

TEN28 PUBLISHING

Hello reader!

While *Off the Stick* is a complete standalone novel, I do have a very special bonus prequel for you.

Before you begin reading this ebook, you can download Halle and Dane's initial meet-cute and steamy short holiday romance in Hockey Boy Holiday. Either use the QR code below or go to: https://BookHip.com/TPRWKHQ

This QR code will take you to a BookFunnel page where you can download the FREE prequel

1

———

A^x "It's an undeniable fact that women love hockey butts."

The entire locker room erupts in loads of uproarious laughter at the comment made by Cale Costa, our team's captain. It's in response to yet another ridiculous and off-the-wall question asked by Tanner Rossco, one of our defense men. Rossy, as he's nicknamed, is notorious for bringing up the oddest topics post-practice and -game, when we're all sweaty and gross and in need of showers.

Last week we had an assortment of oddities, including why do fish taste "fishy" and why are there funny terms for hockey hair and mustaches but not beards. He has a point—I've spent way too much time trying to think of another word for beard. Can't do it.

But tonight's question to the boys is why women watch hockey, and that one's resulted in a host of responses, including one from Wyatt Pedergast, who happens to be our only openly gay player on the team.

He stands up from the bench, turns around, and twerks his towel-covered ass. "I'd also like to point out that some men appreciate 'em too."

This produces a few more hoots from the guys as they chime in to indicate their agreement on the topic. Someone bellows, "It's not as good as mine, Pedey!"

Now, as a naked Duncan Brewer walks in from the showers with a towel draped over his shoulder, he shakes his head—and his dick—and offers up another response in this absurd conversation. "Nah, bruh. We all know why women love hockey players." He stops smack dab in the middle of the room and cups his junk in his hand. "It's obviously because of the way we handle our sticks."

A few dirty towels are thrown at Brewsky, and he ducks out of the way with a deep cackle of a laugh.

I smirk at my fellow forward. "Can they even find yours?" He grabs at his crotch again with a grin and flips me off.

"Guys...it's not why they love *players*," Rossy bellows in a frustrated tone. "It's why they love *watching* hockey."

"Same difference," our backup goalie, Deiter Volmer, offers. "They like to watch *us*."

Bending over to remove my shin guards, I toss them into a pile on the floor as I listen to the boys add more ideas to the mix. Each one increases Rossy's frustration and gets him even more riled up than he was.

I finally join in with my two cents, only because I like

to push Rossy's buttons and he's always a good sport about it, dishing it back with his unique retorts and chirps. "Come on, eh? We all know the ladies come to see the fights and sick action on the ice that account for our sexy toothless smiles."

To prove my point, I lift my chin and demonstrate the power of this boyishly charming grin that has had more than a few women swooning. Raising my finger, I tap my front tooth—the fake one that replaced the cracked one. I got that injury when I took a puck to my mouth from an off-the-stick shot during playoffs last season. It's one of the hazards of playing pro hockey. Thank God for health insurance and great dental plans.

"No, no, no," Rossy objects, wagging both hands like a ref to signal his disagreement. "I just read an article in *Sports News Today* that mentioned a survey where hockey was listed as the top sport women love to watch. It's because of all the social media attention and this thing called BookTok or something."

He rolls back his shoulders, looking overly proud of himself for this next fact. "Sexy hockey romance books are all the rage and have caused an insurgence in female viewership."

Raising my eyebrows, I peer up from unlacing my skates and shake my head at his word choice error, then go back to my task.

"Rossy, I'm never sure exactly what the fuck you're talking about because you're an idiot, but I'm fairly certain you mean *resurgence*, not *insurgence*," quips our

Harvard-graduated six-foot-six center, Oli "Thorny" Thornquist, in that soft-spoken manner of his. "Two very different meanings."

The guys all light up in laughter—even though half of them probably didn't even catch the error.

But Rossy doesn't seem to care that he was just called out in front of his team. He just shrugs it off and gives the double bird to Thorny. "Whatever, bruh. *You* know what I meant."

The locker room fills with *not really, dude, not a clue,* and *you're an idiot, bruh.*

Being one of our D-men, Rossy has moved up the ranks and assumed the line position Ballas Keeney vacated when he recently moved into the role of team GM. There is no denying that Rossy is a fucking great player, but no one has ever accused him of being the brightest bulb in the box.

"The bigger and more pressing question here," Costa adds as he slathers on some aftershave, "is, who knew you could even read, Rossy? *That* is news."

Rossy scoffs and throws a towel at Costa's head but misses, the material falling on the ground in front of Cale's skates. Nils Lungren walks by, carrying his freshly sharpened skates, and bends over to pick it up, throwing it back to Rossy, who snatches it in his hand.

"Dude, I'm not as dumb as I look." The statement hangs in the air for a second and then the entire locker room explodes in more laughter. Rossy shakes his head sputtering out in laughter himself. "Wait...*wait*. I meant *you*. I'm not as dumb as YOU look."

But the damage was already done, and there's no coming back from that one. Rossy can be relied on for two things on the team: one, he's one of the best shot blockers and brings a physicality that's unmatched in the league. Second, he's the team's goofball and funny man— a natural class clown borne out of his wacky comments.

Case in point: today's conversation.

All in all, this group of guys, including Rossy and our rookies, have meshed together well throughout preseason workouts and practices. We have a talented line-up with a great mixture of new and old guards. I'm probably considered one of the old guard now that I've played in the NHL for nearly five years, two of them as the Vikings' starting right winger.

This sport and career are about learning to trust and depend on your team. That bond starts in the locker rooms before we even hit the ice.

I slip off my practice jersey and throw it in the laundry basket so our equipment manager can grab it later and get it cleaned. My game day jersey is already hanging up in preparation for the preseason game tonight against LA.

It's the beginning of the new season and we're coming back from our summer vacations refreshed and ready to kick ass and work our way back to the playoffs. Last year was hard fought but we just couldn't make it happen in the end.

That's life when you're playing in the big leagues. You need the magic and team dynamic to win. It also requires elite players who forge a relationship on and off the ice and a bit of the hockey gods' favor to achieve team success.

"Sure, bruh," I chuckle, slipping my pads over my shoulders to hang them up. "Whatever you say. You don't have to try to convince us of anything."

The chirps, jabs and banter continue for a while longer as the team goes about our post-practice hygiene rituals before we head out for personal time before the game.

Since I felt a crimp develop in my left shoulder blade today, I head to where our massage therapist Kip is working on the guys. I'm hoping some soft tissue work will loosen things up before tonight. I got hit hard into the boards during our last game and it's been giving me hell ever since.

I suppose I've been luckier than most when it comes to injuries. Aside from a few minor sprains and bruises here and there—and the broken front tooth last season—I've not suffered the same consequences that my teammates have endured from playing this sport. It can really beat a guy up.

Taking survey of the room while I wait for Kip to finish with Brett Cannfield, another Vikings D-man, I note the number of guys who have had surgeries and been out for weeks or sometimes months as they recover.

Soren "Wolf" Wolfenspiel, our goalie, was laid up

with a major groin injury. That one sucked because Volmer isn't as lithe as Soren. That man pounces on a puck like a wolf on its prey. But damn, groin injuries are no joke. A guy can't even have sex for at least six weeks during the recovery period.

Jesus, how would I ever survive that? Hopefully, I'll never have to find out.

Then there's Costa, who's probably my best friend on the team and my partner-in-crime forward and 2-way winger, who had knee surgery two years ago and is just getting back to where he left off. I teased that he *Costa'd* us a lot of games during his recovery period. He didn't think it was so funny.

And Cannfield, or Canners as we call him, had a concussion that kept him out of multiple games last season.

I take a seat to wait, feeling lucky about my nonspecific injuries. Knock wood.

Outside of the injuries that set us back a little in the standings, I couldn't be happier with the great team of guys I'm playing with right now. We've all gelled and work well together out on the ice. And we all get along off the ice, too. With Ballas at the helm as our GM, and Coach Thomas and his strong coaching staff, I honestly believe we have a shot at the championship this year.

Wouldn't that be fucking nice? After being on the Chicago team, where we were the worst in the league, I helped get the Vikings into the playoffs my first season here.

I'm surfing my phone, still waiting for a massage and thinking about last season, when Grant Theroux, our assistant coach, walks into the center of the room, completely in team gear. He looks like a walking billboard for Vikings-style men's fashion.

"Alright boys, listen up. Coach T has called a team meeting. You've got five minutes to finish up and get your asses in chairs."

Groans and curses can be heard around the locker room as Coach Theroux leaves, the door banging behind him.

"Fuck, man. There go my plans," laments Canners, who hastily jumps off the table and reaches for his shorts, pulling his phone out from his pocket. "I still need to pick out a gift for Jeanette before I get home. It's our ten-year anniversary, and we're going out after the game to celebrate."

"Someone's not gonna get laid tonight," Volmer chirps as he walks by.

I stride by and thump his back with my palm. "Sucks to be you, bro. That's why I don't have a wife or a girlfriend. I don't need anyone being mad at me for putting hockey first."

Canners scowls. "Someday, Ax, you'll want just that. Your priorities will change when the right woman comes along."

"Whatever you say, Canners. But don't hold your breath."

2

———

Halle

"Welcome to the Vancouver Vikings organization, Halle."

My new boss, Trevor Wilkes, greets me warmly with a bright smile affixed to his mustached face as he shakes my hand. I exhale the breath I'd been holding since walking into the building this morning and return his smile.

"How was the move? Did you get settled in okay?"

I nod, absently rubbing my lower back. Somehow, even after my two younger brothers did most of the heavy lifting, I managed to tweak it while moving furniture into my new place this past weekend. And that was the easy part.

The tough part was the over-ten-hour drive between Calgary and Vancouver while trying to keep my ever rambunctious and physically active daughter Lennon entertained, fed, and focused on anything other than the words, *are we there yet? It's been ages*. My daughter seems to think anything that takes longer than five minutes is ages.

"Thank you, Trevor. The move was not without its complications, but I'm so excited to finally be here. It's seriously a dream come true."

And that is not an understatement. Getting a job with the Vikings organization is something I still can't believe happened.

With a sweep of his arm, Trevor gestures for me to enter and take a seat in his office. I step inside and sit across from him at a small conference table. "Let's get all the paperwork out of the way so we can do a tour of the admin offices, introduce you to everyone, and show you the team facility. Then I get to put you to work."

Inhaling deeply, I exhale the anxiety that's been building since I accepted the offer with the Vikings last month. As Trevor fiddles with some paperwork, I take in his office decor. It's exactly like I expected it to be—decorated with pennants, photos, encased jerseys, and various other hockey memorabilia from both his stint as a pro hockey player and his current position as part of Vikings management.

Trevor Wilkes was a known entity to me long before I first interviewed with him. In fact, one of my brothers —I think it was Zack—had Trevor's poster, the one from his Toronto-playing era, tacked up to his wall for years.

But never in a million years would I have ever expected I would someday be working for him.

I keep wanting to pinch myself in case it's all a dream. It all happened in such a rush; I barely had time to consider the endgame. Or the potential drawbacks of accepting this position with the Vikings and moving to Vancouver.

This is my first real job using my college major as a junior analyst. It's also the first time I've lived away from my family and my childhood home, not including my short stint in a college dorm in Montana five years ago. This whole situation has me adulting so hard it makes me want to vomit.

But I put those worries aside and focus on the reality of what this will mean for my career. When I finished my degree in sports analytics and management, my goal was to someday be in Trevor's position. I've been around sports all my life. My dad and younger brothers played hockey, and I originally went to university on a volleyball scholarship. Sports is the only thing I've ever wanted to be in.

And someday, I'm going to work my way to the top of this organization.

But first things first. Which right now means onboarding and completing my new employee paperwork.

Trevor pulls out a stack of papers, and the movement bumps the pen next to him, sending it rolling off the table.

"I'll get it," I say, leaning down to pick up the pen and then wincing when I see the shoes I wore today. I wanted to look professional and make a good first impression. So instead of comfortable flats or sneakers, I chose heels that matched my pencil skirt and blazer.

Now I feel slightly ridiculous. This is a sports organization, after all; employees are dressed informally everywhere I look. Even Trevor is in track pants and a long-sleeved pullover that sports a Viking emblem.

Trevor sets the manila envelope labeled *Halle A. MacAlister* aside and places the papers and other items on the table between us. I place the Vikings logo pen in front of me, expecting I'll be putting it to use in a moment.

"You'll find all the standard new employee documents to get you set up with payroll and our security and IT systems. I have you scheduled to meet with a member of the Benefits team this afternoon after lunch, and you'll get a picture taken for your permanent badge. But for now, you'll have an access card to get you inside the building and all the facilities."

On top of the paperwork is a cream-colored fob the size of a credit card, a lanyard with the Vikings team logo attached to it. My stomach shimmies with excitement, like a Bollywood dancer in the movies I've watched. I've officially become an employee of the Vancouver Vikings.

A professional hockey team.

The very same team Dane Axelrod plays on.

It's the only drawback of my otherwise perfect dream job.

I swallow down the lump that's suddenly formed in my throat and remind myself that the likelihood of running into him is slim. So. Very. Slim.

In fact, he'll likely never know I even work here. The reports I run will be funneled through the coaching staff, the only identifiers being my first initial and last name.

In my new role, I'm a junior analyst and data engineer for the hockey operations department, which will keep me buried in the databases, pulling and crunching numbers and analyzing player stats. I'll most likely be confined to a cubicle in the team offices—far, *far* away from where the players practice or the locker rooms and meeting areas dedicated to the team activities.

Trevor explained to me during my second interview that I would rarely, if ever, be asked to attend a game in a formal function. That's left to our video guy, Sanjay. He explained that I would be cross-trained to assist if the need ever arose, but otherwise, my butt is planted at a desk, hidden away from comings and goings of the players and coaches.

The likelihood of me coming face-to-face with my daughter's biological father in my new job with the team is statistically improbable.

Or close to it, anyhow.

"Why don't you get started on these," Trevor says, tapping the paper-clipped stack just as his desk phone rings and his mobile chirps with an incoming text notification. He glances down at his cell and then pushes up from his chair, leaning across the desk to grab the ringing phone, his index finger up in the air. "Sorry for the interruption. Hold on for just a second."

While I wait, I slip the lanyard over my head and flip it around to lay flat against my chest, marveling at how professional it makes me feel. My first-day nerves have settled a little bit now that I've spoken with Trevor, who has put me at ease in a way I hadn't expected. He's such a kind man. If I had to guess, knowing he played hockey more than twenty years ago, I'd put him around the age of my dad.

"Wilkes here," he says in a pleasant tone. I try to busy myself and remain occupied with something other than eavesdropping in on his conversation.

I glance around the office, getting a sense for who Trevor is based on the collection of photos and plaques on the walls. One of them is from last season and includes the entire team, coaching staff, and back-office support personnel. My gaze immediately zooms in on the brilliant smile of #25.

He's hard to miss. He's six-feet tall with light sandy-blond hair cut a bit shorter around the ears and longer on the top. The front of his hair flops dramatically over to one side, and he wears a boyishly adorable grin that emphasizes the dimple in the cleft of his chin.

My heart flips inside my chest, and I mentally chastise myself for being so easily distracted by those handsome features.

Trevor's voice goes quiet for a moment, so I turn back and see him plop into his desk chair. "Mm-hmm ...

okay … got it. Last year's SAT report. You bet. We'll be right down."

I watch with increasing interest as Trevor hurriedly types on his keyboard, after which the printer next to his desk comes to life with a few beeps and hisses, and several pages spit out into a tray.

He stands up and reaches for the printouts, shuffling through each with a perfunctory glance before peering up at me.

"Okay, MacAlister. Change of plans. You're coming with me," he states matter-of-factly, using the papers in his hand to gesture for me to stand up. "We're heading down to drop these off with Coach Thomas for his team meeting."

Another thrill of excitement whooshes through me as the reality of all this truly hits. I'm about to meet Head Coach Conner Thomas in the flesh. I'm sure my brothers will pester me for all the details and pepper me with questions when I talk to them tonight. To say that we are a hockey family is like calling the Trudeau's Canadian political royalty.

My brothers, Zack and Drew eat, sleep, and breathe hockey. There hasn't been a moment in their lives when they weren't immersed in the sport. My dad had been passionate about the game since childhood, played in high school and college, and got both boys into playing as soon as they could. I gave it a try as a kid but never enjoyed the ice, so I stuck to other sports.

Although I stopped playing it early in my life, I still loved to watch hockey and root my brothers on.

I was sixteen when my mom succumbed to a short battle with cancer, and the rest of my high school career was spent chauffeuring the boys, just like my mom had once done, around my own extracurricular activities. Hockey was the glue that held us all together after my mom died.

If the boys weren't playing the sport, they were watching it, obsessing over every aspect they could—which is why I'm so knowledgeable on the players and stats of each team. It was the way I connected with my brothers and my dad. It also helps that I'm a stats nerd and love talking numbers.

Hockey was what lead me to sports analytics and is the reason I chose a career in this field. The only applications I sent in were for open positions with all levels of professional hockey teams.

And when, after three rounds of intensive interviews, I accepted this position, the encouragement my dad and brothers gave me was amazing. It lessened the fear I felt from leaving everything behind in Calgary and starting a new career and life as working single mom in Vancouver.

And it assuaged the guilt I felt for taking my daughter Lennon away from the only family she'd ever known.

I ignore the stabbing sensation in my heart and push to my feet to follow Trevor out the door. He easily navigates the maze of desks and cubicles and then down a long corridor while I follow behind like a lost puppy.

When he pushes the elevator button for Up, I realize we're not going to Coach Thomas's office.

From the final in-person interview I had when he briefly showed me around the office, I know the coaching staff and leadership team offices are all on this floor, just further down the hallway and in a more privately secure area.

As we wait for the lift to arrive, I remain quiet and stare at each of the framed promo posters that line the walls on both sides of us. There's one of the Vikings' captain, Cale Costa, D-man Tanner Rossco, forward Nils Lundren, and our starting goalie, Soren "The Wolf" Wolfenspiel.

The elevator doors open on a whoosh and I glance down at my feet before stepping in to make sure I don't get my heel stuck in the crevasse. When I look back up, I come face-to-face with a blast from my past.

Or at least, the framed image of number twenty-five, Dane "Ax" Axelrod. Larger than life, as is the divot in the middle of his chin.

The same one Lenni has on her cherub face.

I practically stumble onto the lift, and Trevor catches me by my arm to steady me. "Whoa there, MacAlister. Watch your step." He lets go but looks to be at the ready in the event I keel over, nodding his chin down to my feet with a smile. "Maybe tomorrow leave the heels at home. No need for them here."

I gather my balance and chuckle. "Yeah, I'm much better in my running shoes. Heels are a killer."

He nods in understanding, and the doors close in front of us.

"My wife, Lizzie, would agree with you. But my nineteen-year-old daughter lives for those ankle-breakers," he adds with a laugh. Then his voice turns from humor to compassionate. "Which reminds me, did you get your daughter enrolled in the on-site daycare program?"

My head snaps up to my new boss, who looks down upon me with such a tender expression that I could easily burst out in tears of emotion.

Had it not been for Trevor, who let me know in my second interview about the generous benefit offered to Vikings employees, players, and staff, I wouldn't have even considered accepting this job. In fact, I was going to decline any further interviews for fear I was in way over my head and wouldn't have any options for Lenni.

But the Little Vikings on-site daycare program meant that Lenni would be right here in the facility with me during work hours, and it's affordable for all employees. That one benefit alone is a career-making opportunity, offering me the incentive I needed to spread my wings and leave the nest, so to speak. I no longer had to put any more burden on my dad to help care for my daughter.

Being a working single mom is tough enough, but it's nearly impossible without family nearby or the child's father to help. One last look behind me at the picture of Dane has my heart squeezing inside my chest as I think about all the single moms who break their backs daily to raise their kids alone.

I nod appreciatively at Trevor. "Yes. Thank you so much. Lennon is so excited to start at Little Vikings on Monday. Until then, my dad is here to help us get settled."

"That's great, I'm so happy to hear that." He smiles congenially. "But you don't have to thank me. It was Karis Spurlock, the team owner, who came up with that benefit program and worked out the budget to prioritize it for staff and team alike. In fact, you'll get to meet Karis after this meeting."

Suddenly, the idea of meeting not only Coach Thomas but also Karis Spurlock in the flesh has my heart racing faster than a flying puck toward the plexiglass. Sweat beads under my armpits and seeps through my brand-new blouse.

I've gone down more than one internet rabbit hole about the Vikings owner, Karis Spurlock. I've read—and empathized with her from afar—about the death of her uncle, the family tragedy that led her to taking on the ownership of the team. I've heard about the adversity and severe misogyny she encountered at the male-dominated leadership tables within the league—and how she single-handedly made swift and sweeping changes within her own organization to drive out the sexism and chauvinistic behavior that existed.

In a nutshell, she is one badass boss lady and my idol.

Trying not to shake with excitement too much, I follow closely behind as Trevor winds around a corner and stops in front of a set of double doors. He places a hand on the door handle, rolls his shoulders back, and gives me a look.

"You ready, MacAlister?" he asks. Then he smiles and winks before opening the door. "Nothing like jumping right into the deep end your first day on the job."

I'm not exactly sure what to expect until he swings open the door, waving me in before him, and I step inside. I nod my thanks and walk on through, then find myself in the front of a large auditorium filled with Vikings hockey players. Who seem to all stop talking at once and stare back at me.

I freeze like I'm caught in a tractor beam.

Holy shit. The entire Vikings team is looking at me like I'm a newborn elephant at the local zoo.

Trevor quickly adjusts and agilely sidesteps me, giving me a surreptitious, supportive grin over his shoulder. He heads toward a front table where all the coaches are seated. Finally snapping out of my daze, I move in, trying to covertly hide myself, and then stumble into his back. Because— gah— the high heels! Trevor pivots, his hands clutching my shoulders to stabilize me before he turns back around, and I'm left to feel like a complete idiot.

My eyes dart around for the nearest trash can. I wonder if I can make it to a bathroom to vomit or just heave right now, in front of a room full of eyes staring down at me. I imagine this is why possums play dead when frightened. I want to curl up in a ball and hide from embarrassment. My hands tremble as I lift my gaze and dare another glance out at the sea of faces.

And I blanch.

If someone asked me how I expected my first day to go, I would've said it'd probably be boring as hell, with all my time devoted to filling out paperwork and reading a new-hire training manual.

It would not have included standing in front of some of the best and most celebrated players in the league and making a complete ass of myself.

Okay, maybe I'm being slightly overdramatic. If I had a highlight reel to look back on the events of today, I'm sure I'll realize it wasn't that big of a deal and have a good laugh at myself. In fact, as I scan the room, most of the audience has lost interest and are quietly talking amongst themselves, looking at their phones, or centering their attention on the coach and Trevor. They aren't concerned about little ol' me in the slightest.

Except maybe for one pair of eyes that is laser-focused on me.

The pair I last saw five over years ago.

Dane Axelrod.

Dane's dark, steel-gray gaze is locked squarely on mine and filled with confusion. Does he recognize me? Or maybe he's wondering to himself why I look familiar? That phenomenon when you see someone out of context and can't quite place them.

Or it could be something else entirely. Maybe it's a look of displeasure, and he's not happy to see me at all.

Whatever the reason for his strange expression, it's disconcerting that he won't quit staring at me. His eyebrows furrow, and he tilts his head side to side.

What is he thinking about? If he does remember me, I'm sure he's recalling the last time we spoke. The night I called things off between us. I mean, our break-up was amicable. We agreed to go our separate ways, no harm, no foul. I even reached out via text to send my heartfelt congratulations the day he got drafted: *You did it, Ax. I'm so happy for you.*

If either one of us has just cause to be angry, it's me. He never texted so much as a thank-you back. Honestly, though, it's not like I expected to hear from him again.

Dane was busy being celebrated as the newest sensation in the show, touted as one of the next best rookies in the league, and I was just the girl he had a short fling with six months earlier.

I'm sure I'm the last person on earth he ever thought he'd see walking into a Vikings team meeting. After all, I definitely didn't think I'd be in the middle of this auditorium on my first day.

That one sure wasn't on my new-hire bingo card.

3

A^x

Holy shit.

The last thing I expected at a post-practice meeting was to see Halle MacAlister.

The girl— um, and now *very* hot businesswoman— who gave up on us—on me—over five years ago. The one I never quite got over.

A grueling practice had already taken the wind out of me, but her unexpected appearance knocks me on my fucking ass. If I weren't already in a chair, I might have collapsed at seeing her in the flesh. Surprise, confusion, and longing hit me hard when I realize it's her.

What in the fuck is my ex doing in Vancouver?

Cherry.

The last time we spoke was six months before I was drafted. We'd spent the better part of that December and January together. It was our last night together, and we were sitting in my car, trying to keep warm in the frigid Calgary winter.

"Dane... I think we need to say goodbye... It just won't work with us being so far away... Let's just part friends."

Even at eighteen, I knew she was making sense, that this was the best thing for us to do. We were going in different directions—she was leaving for college in the States, and I was going into the draft that June. Our romance had been intense and short-lived, but the relationship was over before it even began.

But knowing that still didn't stop my heart from breaking when she left me that night and I never heard from her again. Since then, I've chosen not to get close to another woman. I don't want to stick my heart out on my sleeve only for it to be iced. I've decided to live free and easy, enjoying the company of women without the hassles of getting involved. Some might call me a player off the ice, but honestly, it's out of self-preservation.

If I couldn't be with Halle, I didn't want to be with anyone.

"I wish we had more time, Cherry," I murmur, my lips *finding the soft warm skin of her neck. "I wish..."*

"Just promise me you won't forget me, Dane."

And to this day, I never have. She left a hole in my empty heart that I've never tried to fill again. I suppose you could say I went off the rails in terms of the number of women I've been with. Since that frigid January night, I only want to have a good time and not get hooked.

From his seat next to me, Thorny elbows me in the

ribs, bringing me back to the present. Rubbing the spot, I swing my head toward him and grumble, "What the fuck, bruh?"

His look telegraphs *What's wrong with you, bro*, and he gestures with the universal signal to shut up. "Pipe down, bruh. You just said cherry super loud."

I blink, realizing that a few of the guys have all turned around and are staring at me like I've totally lost my mind. Jesus, maybe I have? I've barely heard anything Coach has said in the past five minutes. My ears ring like I just got body-checked into the boards and thrown down on the ice.

When I look back to the front of the room, I intentionally lock my eyes on Karis, our team owner, and tell myself to *focus, goddammit*. She's talking about some changes on the leadership staff and upcoming community events that need team representation from some of us players.

Karis begins rattling off event names, dates, and the players assigned to each one. I cringe and my head lolls forward when she reads off my name for some interview podcast. Thorny makes a noise at the back of his throat, and I throw him a glare.

"Seems like I skated past that one," he snickers in my ear. "She obviously wants only the camera-ready smiles and those who don't whistle when they speak. And we all know that ain't me."

I flip him off, but Thorny smiles maniacally, exposing the gap from a missing front tooth.

"You got that right," I murmur, and feel him laughing silently next to me.

Costa, Thorny, Rossy and Wolf have been the guys I've hung out with quite a bit in the past year. Since there are only a handful of single guys on the team, they make for good wingmen out at the bars when we go out. Well, except for Wolf. He's as grumpy as they come, and he never says much unless it's a curse in German, which we can never understand.

Thorny and I also played a lot of golf together last summer, along with Ballas Keeney, who would join us when he could get away from the new day job. Rossy wisely stayed off the course because he sucks at golf, and Wolf disappeared for the majority of the summer and went back to Austria to visit his family.

Karis ends her speech and leaves the stage to a round of applause, waving at us as she heads off, and Coach returns to the podium. He discusses strategies and line assignments for tonight's game, then briefly turns to chat with Trevor Wilkes.

"Team, I want to introduce you to our newest staff member, Halle MacAlister." He gestures with an outstretched arm to Halle, who looks more than a little shell-shocked from her place behind Trevor. "Halle will be responsible for collecting and analyzing all the team's available data. Welcome aboard our Vikings ship, Halle."

Applause and the team's *Skol* chant erupt through the room. I see a red blush spread over Halle's neck and face.

Thorny gives a low whistle and leans close to my ear.

"Damn, who knew data nerds were so damn hot?" My hand darts out instinctively, and I punch his chest. He rubs a palm over the spot. "*Fuuuck*, bro… that hurt."

An instinctive, possessive growl erupts from my chest. "Not cool, Thorn. Show some respect."

He sniffs and lets out a low grumble. "Whatevs, dude. Like you weren't thinking the same thing."

My gaze remains laser-focused on Cherry. I've never seen her looking so professional and put together before. When we dated, she was always in hoodies and jeans. Or naked with me.

I shake that mental image free from my head to avoid sporting a stiffy; this is not the setting for that.

Okay, so maybe I was thinking the same thing Thorny was—she is breathtaking in her tailored suit. But I can go down that path because Halle and I have history together. I know things about her that no one else knows.

I was Halle's first. We shared something together that no one else can ever repeat.

My thoughts jump from the past to the present, and a mess of confusion and questions jumble in my head.

What is Halle doing here? I don't understand.

I never expected to see Cherry again, and definitely not under these circumstances. Here. In Vancouver. Working for the same team I play for.

Did fate just pass me a second chance with the one girl I let get away?

4

Halle

There's nothing more luxurious than taking a long, hot bath without interruption.

I'm taking advantage of these last few days of his built-in support before my Dad leaves next week. After he's gone, it'll be the first time since Lenni was born that I'll truly be raising her on my own.

The thought fills me with excitement and a little bit of dread.

I worry about whether I'm strong enough to do this all on my own, if I've possibly made a mistake moving away from home, even if it is for my dream job.

When I first told Dad I was pregnant, I was of course worried about his response. I was, after all, his only daughter. It was understandable that he might be upset over my decision and would try to talk me out of keeping my child, since he and Mom had both been very young when they had me. Had my mom still been alive, would she have been in my corner? Or convinced me to give the baby up and finish college.

All my concerns were unfounded. Dad jumped in with his whole heart and has been there for me and Lenni every step of the way.

Although I initially never told him the baby was Dane's, Dad figured it out but never pressured me about it. He knew about my relationship with Dane before I left for college, and the timing of the pregnancy pointed directly at Dane as the father of my child.

But because my father is who he is, even with all his shortcomings and the long absences away from his family as a truck driver, he did everything he could to step up, becoming my rock and the father figure Lenni needed in her formative years.

Even Zack and Drew rose to the occasion. They were thrilled to become uncles and fell in love with Lenni the minute they saw her. My daughter has no lack of love in her life.

It didn't prevent me from having difficult days along the way, though. There hasn't been a day that's gone by when I haven't second-guessed my decision to keep Dane in the dark about his daughter's existence or questioned whether my choice was fair to Lenni.

There were moments when I nearly broken down and thought about tracking Dane down to tell him the truth, if only to see if he'd be the kind of stand-up guy Lenni needed as a father.

But every time I came close, I would read something about Dane's off-the-ice behavior and playboy activities, and it stopped me short. I didn't trust that he was capable of settling down and could be relied upon to put Lenni first. Family ties are a priority for me and with how easily Dane let me go in the past, I wasn't going to risk that he'd do the same thing with Lenni.

She's only inquired a few times, but each time she mentions her daddy, it nails me, and sends me in a spiral over whether I made the right decision. But I just don't trust him to be what she needs right now. Maybe ever.

I rub a palm over an ache in my chest and sink further down into the bathtub. The hot water cocoons me in its delicious citrus, honey, and lavender scent. A soapy bubble floats on top of the steamy water, and I pop it with my finger, wishing it was that easy to absolve the anxiety and guilt that bubbles up in my soul. If only my worries would evaporate and fade as easily as bath bubbles.

I just wasn't prepared to see Dane again. Logically, I knew there was a chance since we now work for the same organization. But it was more unsettling then I expected, and a curveball distraction to the excitement I'd been feeling over my new job.

I thought I'd have time to adjust and get ready for that potential run-in. Yet fate had me confronting my past within my first few hours on the job.

Good Lord, I was afraid I'd faint on the spot the moment my eyes connected with his. Everything was a blur, and my nerves had me in a state of panic, but I swear I saw him mouth the word *Cherry*.

But that's probably just foolish thinking on my part.

In the real world, Dane probably forgot about me the moment I left his orbit and had no idea who I was when he saw me today.

I've changed considerably since having a baby. So has Dane. He's grown from an adolescent boy into a full-fledged man. A strange thread of awareness had pulsed through my veins when I caught him staring at me with those unforgettable piercing gray eyes. Even with his still damp hair slicked away from his forehead, and appearing darker than its usual sandy-blond coloring, he was easily recognizable. My heart knew instantly.

And the mass of dark stubble at his cut jawline, new since we last met, spiked that awareness even more.

The sight of Dane in the flesh had my knees weak and my heart pounding. I had wanted to turn and run but wasn't sure my feet could move.

In fact, Trevor had to prod me forward, front and center, when Coach Thomas introduced me as the newbie—to the entire freaking team! I was so self-conscious that heat rose up my neck and to my cheeks.

It felt like Coach would never stop talking, but when he did, I dared to peek back up, my gaze landing squarely on Dane.

Who grimaced, his brows drawn together.

He may not have remembered me at first sight, but he

had to have put two and two together when Coach Thomas said my name.

And the frown that marred his face suggested he was pissed that I was there.

But why? What could I have done to make him angry?

He was the one who never even bothered to respond to my text after the draft that year. Not even a quick hello or thank-you, which only helps prove my case that Lenni and I are better off without him. We'd never come first. He was quick to dismiss me from his life then, and it wouldn't be any different now.

Dane Axelrod disappeared from my life like a popped bubble and took my heart with him. After that, I blocked his number.

I had to do that to keep myself from ever contacting him again and prevent him from potentially asserting himself back into my life.

As if that would ever happen.

Ax became a touted rookie with Chicago and was then traded to the Vikings. There was no way he was ever going to find room in his life for Lenni.

Or me.

A tiny knock on the door draws me out of my self-pity, and I force a smile on my face.

"Come in."

The door handle wiggles, sticks, then jiggles again, and finally Lenni's face appears through a crack.

"Hi, Mama," she says in that cute little voice of hers.

"Papa said it's time for bed, but I want you to wead me a bedtime story."

Lenni steps into the small bathroom, wearing her pink Disney princess nightgown—washed earlier today by Dad—the bottom hem swishing around her bare feet. I extend my hand, and she moves forward to clutch it with her tiny one. The pink of her nail polish, done during our nail painting and pizza party the night we moved in, is already chipping away.

I was honestly a bit worried that Lenni would have a tough time moving to Vancouver and leaving behind all that was familiar to her, including her obnoxious but loving uncles. Like me, Lenni is reserved when it comes to new things or people; it takes us a while to adapt to new situations. It took her a good two weeks at her last preschool to warm up to her new teacher and a month before she finally made friends.

Dad has been our saving grace at making this entire transition seamless and easy for both of us. He insists that it's only fair, a form of payback for all the years I took care of our home when he was on the road.

It's going to hit like a bucket of cold water when he leaves for Calgary and reality comes at us full force.

Then it'll just be her and me.

I stretch across the porcelain tub to place a kiss on Lenni's knuckles. Ripples of water splash over the side as I do and bubbles float in the air, drawing a giggle from my sweet girl.

"Okay, I can do that. Ask Papa to help you pick out a

book and get you tucked in bed, and I'll be there in five minutes."

She nods and sprints out into the hallway, leaving the door ajar so the warm air of my spa-like bathroom seeps out.

I sink back down into the deliciously scented water and sigh. A mother's job is never done.

And I wouldn't have my life any other way. Lenni is the best decision I ever made, and I know my own mother is looking down from heaven with a smile on her face.

I just hope I can manage the responsibility of parenting on my own while working full time and also navigating the possibility of seeing my ex again.

But for now, my brain can only handle one thing at a time. And that's leaving the warmth of the bath and putting my daughter to bed with a story.

5

A^x

"Are you going out with us tonight, Ax?"

I shrug noncommittally at Rossy's question as we exit Vegas's visiting team locker room.

Our preseason game against the Vanguards ended in a satisfying overtime win for us, with Lundy making the goal from my assist to save us from going into overtime. It was a fantastic shot, and most of the guys are eager to head to the Strip, where someone's assistant has already reserved a private room for us at Club Aces.

Under normal circumstances, I'd have been more than happy to go celebrate. In fact, the last time we were in Vegas, Cale and I had a smokin' hot threesome with a gorgeous and fun-loving showgirl named Katarina. We'll see where the night goes from here, but thanks to Halle showing up in my life earlier this week, my mind has been on my past, not future hookups.

"Yeah, I'll join you for a drink," I reply, checking the time on my phone as we head to the team bus. "Just one, though. Plane leaves at 8 a.m. tomorrow, so I want to be back by midnight."

Rossco throws a beefy arm over my shoulder. He smells of strong cologne and mint.

"Aww, come on, you old lady. We only have a practice tomorrow afternoon at home, which means we have all *niiight* to live it up in Vegas, baby! It's going to be sick, bruh."

"Mm-hmm."

The idea of pulling an all-nighter tonight—especially after three nights in a row of interrupted sleep—doesn't sound the least bit appealing.

I blame Halle MacAlister for those problems. It's because of her I've been suffering from lack of sleep and a lack of interest in getting fucked up and busting a nut with a hot hookup.

All her fault.

My brain still reels over her appearance in Vancouver without any warning. She must've known I play for the Vikings, right? Why didn't she ever contact me to tell me she was here? At the very least, to say, "Hey, Ax. I live in Vancouver now. Want to meet up?"

I guess I can understand why she wouldn't. It's been over five years since we last spoke. She could be married or in a serious relationship and maybe have no interest in seeing me again.

But the mere idea that she would never want to see

me again sends a clawing sensation to my stomach, which clenches and churns like an angry sea in a storm.

There've been many times over the years when I've thought about her, dreamed about her, remembered that last night we had together before we parted ways on our way into adulthood.

At the time, we agreed to part on good terms, no drama, and go our separate ways. Halle's logical explanation was that she didn't want a long-distance relationship with a hockey player.

I get it. Honestly, I probably wasn't mature enough to continue a relationship that stood the test of time across vast distances. It would've ended at some point—right? And probably badly, with resentment and broken hearts on both sides.

I've witnessed some of my closest friends and teammates go through gruesome, and nasty breakups and divorces due to complications that can come with a relationship that includes a professional hockey career. Halle and I agreed that we were both too young to make that type of commitment to each other.

But I still regret that we never gave it a try. We'd been great together and had an inexplicable pull I'd not ever felt before her. Unlike some other girls I met in juniors, Halle liked me for me, not because I was a hockey player. Yet, she loved the sport and completely geeked out over hockey stats.

Those four weeks I spent with Halle had been anything but puppy love. Our time together had been vivid, visceral, and it was a knife to my heart when it ended. It took me a while to deal with the fact I'd probably never see her again.

And then suddenly, five and a half years go by and... Boom. She's alive and well and living here in Vancouver?

Seeing her again brought all those old feelings rushing to the surface and she's been on my mind constantly. It's honestly killing my sleep schedule because of how much she's been appearing in my dreams. It's a wonder I skated as well as I did tonight because I'm exhausted beyond belief.

Which is the reason I shouldn't go out tonight.

Rossy, on the other hand, looks like he's just downed two Red Bulls and snorted a line of coke. Although to be fair, this is his natural state. The dude is like a Labrador puppy, always bouncing like a kid on a trampoline.

Costa thumps my other shoulder with his palm. "I'm going with these idiots. We can skip out together."

"Okay, fine. Let's do it, bro," I finally concede, mainly to get Rossco off my back. I turn to Costa and shrug with an eye roll.

Rossco lets out a hoot of excitement and jabs a fist in the air. "It's gonna be lit, boys! We're in Vegas, baby!"

16 Hours Later

"Get your asses moving, boys! Most of you look like you were dragged in from the back alley today!" Coach

Thomas yells from the middle of the rink, where we've been doing speed drills the past twenty minutes. "This isn't a free skate. We have Florida tomorrow night. No mercy or fucks will be given if you're slagging."

I'm not nearly as hungover as some of my teammates, but I'm still struggling to rid myself of a headache that's been lingering for most of the day. That happens when you're working on less than five hours of sleep, two of which occurred on the plane ride home.

The trip from Vegas back to Vancouver takes less than three hours, but during that time a couple of our rookies, including Case Lyons and Shaw Benning, were in the lavatory hugging the porcelain throne while they puked up the previous night's excessive alcohol. Rookie mistake.

But that wasn't the biggest blunder that happened last night. That mistake was eclipsed by my friend and our team captain, Costa, ended up getting married.

Mother fucking married!

Never in a million years would I have expected a typical night out on the Vegas Strip to end up with me standing as best man for Costa.

Being Vegas, our quick celebration went from low-key to wild when we got invited to join a bachelorette party in progress. Next thing we knew, Cale's getting hitched.

This is the guy who doesn't even order a meal without considering all the options. When he bought his house, it took over a year for him to finally settle on a place, for fuck's sake. But within hours of meeting someone, he ends up married to her?

I'm still in shock over his spontaneous out of character decision. We're currently doing drills at the moment, and as I weave in and out around the cones with the puck, I lift my eyes for the briefest of seconds and catch a dopey-ass grin on Costa's face.

The toe of my stick stutters against the ice, and before I can regain control, the puck veers wildly off course.

"*Fuck*," I gripe, slapping the butt of my stick. I skate off to the side, where the chuckles from the guys along the wall make me even angrier at my loss of concentration.

Coming to a stop next to Costa, I bump his shoulder pad with mine to gain his attention.

"What's up?" he asks casually, looking like he didn't just pull an all-nighter.

"Bro, how can you be so calm right now?"

Should I have stopped him from making this life-altering decision? If the tables were turned, I'd want my best friend to step in and be the voice of reason, right?

Costa shrugs, his eyes scanning the drills taking place around us, and then gives me a look of incredulity, like he doesn't know why I'm asking such a question.

He doesn't even seem the least bit fazed that he is now legally wed to a complete stranger. I asked him three times at the altar if he was sure about what he was about to do.

"It's all good. I'm doing the right thing." That's all he said to me before *getting fucking married*.

I'm still wondering if he really was as sober as he said he was.

I shake my head. "That was a fucking crazy-ass decision you made, don't you think? Why aren't you freaking out right now?"

His green eyes crinkle, and there's a flash of a crooked grin as he lets out a laugh. Then he responds in his typical thoughtful, very Costa-like manner.

"It just seemed like the right thing to do."

"The right thing?" My voice goes up an octave in utter disbelief. His entire attitude is just plain weird. "Did you knock her up or something?"

Costa chuckles. "I don't think it happens that fast."

I mean, okay. A lot of quicky marriages happen during crazy drunken nights in Vegas, but most end once both parties sober up and realize what a mistake they'd made. I figure that's why Vegas also has a high rate of quickie divorces.

But from the sound of it, Cale and his new wife—I don't even know her name, for fuck's sake! —are planning to stay married. I swivel on my skates so I can fully face him, eyeing him with all the skepticism and censure I can dredge up from my emotional bank.

"Dude, you don't know that woman. At. All." I punctuate the last two words with a stick tap on the ice. "She could take you to the fucking cleaners. Or worse, sell you out publicly if things go south. You have major assets and financial interests to protect."

Why I'm so overly invested and concerned about the state of Cale's relationship status is beyond me—Except for that I worry about him getting *married* on a fucking whim. That's a big fucking deal.

I huff out an exasperated breath as I continue to glare at him. He just grins back at me, slipping a glove back over his hand and tapping the top of his stick against my helmet. A whistle blows to indicate a change on the ice, and he pushes off the boards.

"Good talk, buddy," he calls over his shoulder as he skates toward the middle of the ice, where his line mates are circling up. I stare aghast at his nonchalance as he passes around the puck like it's just another day of practice.

My skin suddenly flushes hot, irritation peaking and about to spill over. Why the fuck does it matter to me that he's married?

Maybe it's the fact that he'll no longer be my single friend and wingman. As a married man, he won't want to go out and party with me any longer. Look what happened to Keeners.

That must be the reason I'm so annoyed. Nobody likes to be left behind as their friends partner up. This is all good old-fashioned abandonment issues on my part.

Another whistle blows and Coach wraps up our practice with a quick pep talk before we all head off to the locker rooms.

As I leave the ice, I give myself a mental shake and make a promise I'll get my head back in the fucking game. I should be focusing on playing excellent hockey tonight instead of worrying about Cale's love life.

Or Halle's.

Heading down the tunnel, I deposit my stick and gloves with the assistant equipment manager and head toward the locker room. During this trek, I decide that it's time I track Halle down and confront the elephant in the room—at least, the one that's been taking up headspace for me this past week. I just need to be an adult about it, have a conversation to catch up, find out how she's doing, what's going on in her life now, and then I can get her out of my mind.

Just as I come to that conclusion, Coach Thomas calls out my name.

"Hey, Ax. Ballas wants to see you in his office."

I snap my head toward Coach and wrinkle my forehead. "What the hell for? What'd I do?"

He just shrugs. "Don't know. Guess you'll find out."

Christ. Being called into the GM's office is like getting sent to the principal in high school. It's never a good thing.

Let's just add something else I need to worry about.

6

Halle

I've been in my new job for a week now and I've learned enough to make my head spin and question how I'll ever figure it all out. That aside, and putting away that awkward first-day mishap with the team meeting and Dane, I couldn't be happier to be part of this organization. It's everything I'd hoped it would be.

Speaking of which, the team has been out on the road the last few days and are scheduled to be back in town for tonight's game against Florida. Trevor insisted that I take the team seats for our department tonight so Dad, Lenni, and I could attend before he heads back to Calgary.

I look up from my desktop monitor to check the time. It's getting late in the day, and I have about an hour to finish up what I've been working on before Dad swings by with Lenni. I'd promised them both a tour and to introduce her to the daycare teacher.

I'm about to open a file I was working on earlier when PJ Takatsuka, one of my new coworkers, peers over the cube wall. His dark hair nearly covers his eyes, and he pushes it away behind his ear.

"Hey, Halle," he says in a quiet, almost shy voice, brushing the hair across his forehead again. His gaze flits to my desk, avoiding direct eye contact. If I had to guess, he's a total introvert. "Trevor wants me to show you the SQL report and individual player dashboard I created to track the points scored on power plays and team penalty kills stats. Do you have time now?"

I smile and grab my phone and notepad, glancing at the time one more time. "Sure, PJ. Yeah, I'd love to see what you created."

This earns me a smile, which jostles the tiniest 'stache I've ever seen on a guy's face. For as much hair he has on his head, his lip curtain looks a bit goofy.

Stifling a giggle, I round the corner of the wall and enter his immaculate work area. It's already clear that PJ is a perfectionist. Everything on his desk is neatly in its place, with nothing out of order. I find that somewhat comforting in a way. It tells me that he'll be someone I can count on to get accurate reports when they are needed, unlike one of my classmates in college. That guy did only the bare minimum on group projects and had me carrying the brunt of the workload. It made me madder than a wet cat that he got the same grade I did.

Putting those irritants aside, I pull up the chair next to PJ, who swivels around to his desk and taps out a few keystrokes using only his index fingers. I find it strange that a guy who enters data all day, every day, can only use two of his fingers to type so fast. I won't judge, but I chew on the inside of my lip to keep from commenting on his talent.

I stare over his shoulder at his dual monitors and the crazy busy displays of graphs, stats, and charts. A nervous shiver runs down my spine at the reality of my new situation. Once I'm thoroughly trained, I'll be expected to manage all of these reports and data. I wonder if my tiny-mustache colleague felt the same way when he first started.

"Out of curiosity," I hedge, nervously fiddling with my badge hanging around my neck, "how long did it take you to learn all this?"

PJ's fingers come to an immediate halt, and he snaps his head up to stare at me. This time, he meets my gaze straight on, the mustache moving when he screws up his lips. "What do you mean? It's pretty basic database management. You should know this already."

Wow.

Okay, don't I feel pathetic now. I bristle at the patronizing tone that has me wanting to shrink down in my shoes. Belittled by a guy who looks like he's a twelve-year-old boy. I inhale deeply as I try to figure him out. Maybe he doesn't realize how insensitive his response sounded? I lean back in my chair and offer some grace

—after all, we're both learning to work with one another.

"Well, yeah, but I'm sure you didn't have this all nailed down the first week you started, right?" I lift my hand to wave it at all the information blinking back at us on the monitors.

PJ seems to consider this for a second as he turns back to his screen.

"Yeah, I guess so. It was a long time ago, so now it feels pretty second nature. I'm sure you'll be able to figure it out." He gestures with a dismissive wave over his shoulder and leans forward to point at the monitor in front of him.

While he explains the data to me, I scribble notes on the small notepad and try to keep up with all the information and numbers he points out. For all the lack of empathy he might use in conversation, PJ is actually a decent teacher. He regularly stops throughout his explanations to ask if I have any questions. Which I do.

"Let's say I'm asked to run a query on, oh, I don't know. How about Dane Axelrod's power play goals for last season?" I try to sound nonchalant when I mention Ax's name. I suppose I could have used any number of players, but let's face it, Dane has been on my mind a lot lately. "How do I search for that data?"

It's as if a light flipped on inside PJ's head because he literally beams with enthusiasm over my question.

"It's low-key easy once you know how the page is laid out." He taps the monitor in front of us with his finger, and my eyes follow it to the top of the screen. "You just type in his name right up here to pull up the individual player dashboard."

As if saying his name out loud has summoned some kind of magic, Dane Axelrod materializes in the flesh, his patent smirk popping up above the cube wall inches from us.

My entire body stiffens and I swallow hard, hot flame burning my face. PJ, on the other hand, seems thrilled, his dark eyes widening in surprise. He extends a hand over the top of the monitor to clasp Ax's outstretched one in a bro-shake gesture.

"Hey, Ax. Good to see you, man," PJ greets in the most animated fashion I've witnessed since meeting him. "Nice assist on that buzzer beater the other night."

Dane nods absently in appreciation while his gaze fixes on me. I suck in my bottom lip, wholly unprepared for this moment. My heart races as he cocks his head with boyish charm, the look in his eyes almost a dare.

Tension grows and the air between us crackles. Even PJ seems to notice it; his gaze bounces between Dane and me like he's watching a ping-pong match.

Then, as if realizing I may not know the Vikings player, PJ gestures toward me. "Oh, let me introduce you —" he starts, but is interrupted by Dane.

"Hello, Cherry." His words vibrate from his chest.

That gorgeous smile of his that accentuates his chin dimple cuts from cheek to cheek. I notice he hasn't shaved, and coarse stubble the color of golden wheat covers the planes of his sharp jawline. Dane lifts a theatrical brow—full of mischief and danger—like he knows something that everyone else doesn't.

Great. *Just great.*

The use of that sugar-sweet nickname he bestowed upon me is clearly an indicator he remembers me. The day we met, one of the most embarrassing days of my life to that point, I was covered in sticky cherry slushie syrup.

But I'm not that girl anymore. And I won't fall for his boyishly cute charm ever again.

Been there. Done that.

Have the nearly five-year-old to prove it.

PJ gives me a puzzled look, as if trying to calculate things in his head and not making sense of it. "Do you two know each other already?"

I reply, "No."

At the same time, Dane says, "Oh yeah. We go way back."

He leans over the cubicle wall, positioning his bent arms over the top, and props his chin on his hands.

"And we need to catch up. Don't we, Cherry?"

A weird-sounding exhalation gurgles up from my throat, like I've been caught doing something I shouldn't have been. I suck in my lower lip as Dane's eyes latch onto my mouth.

I lift a hand in an awkward wave. "Uh, hey Dane."

PJ's gaze continues to go back and forth, his facial expression telling me he's doing the math but his two plus two isn't equaling four.

"Cherry?" he asks, looking squarely at me.

My words get caught in my throat, my heart thudding so loudly I worry they can hear it. If possible, my face flushes even more—I'm mortified that Dane would use that name in front of my new colleague. But I do work for a hockey team, after all, and hockey players are notorious for giving nicknames to their teammates. As long as Dane doesn't offer the story of how he came up with that name, I'll be fine.

But I'm not one of Dane's teammates. I'm an ex he hasn't seen in five years, and we are in an extremely awkward reunion moment. I flit a hand in the air and hope that Dane will move along so we can avoid any further weirdness.

But the universe is totally against me today. As luck would have it, the elevator chimes and little-girl giggles fill the awkward silence that's fallen over the three of us. Giggles followed by my dad's booming voice echoing down the hallway.

"Hold up, kiddo. Wait for Papa."

All eyes turn toward the elevator bank and short corridor not twenty feet away from where we stand, and we see my daughter race at full speed, head down as she shoots toward us.

Right into Dane.

7

In the five years I've played in the pros, I've been hip-checked against the boards, blown up on the ice, and had one of my front chiclets knocked out.

But I have never been pummeled by a pint-sized little girl.

"Whoa there," I say with a laugh. I stagger back on my feet, instinctively and covertly cupping my crotch to protect my balls. Once I know they're not in danger from being badly injured, I reach down and gently grasp the shoulders of a tiny girl who barely reaches past my knees.

She looks up at me, all wide gray eyes and heart-shaped mouth, and giggles. "Oops! Saw-wie, mithter."

It takes me a second to translate the words, giving time for Halle to speedily round the corner and push in front of me.

"Lenni! Be careful!" Halle grabs hold of the little girl's hand and tugs her to her side, then looks at me in distress. She places a hand on my arm, offering an apology. "Dane, I'm so sorry. Are you okay?"

The touch sends an electric current up my spine so powerful it's a shock to my system.

Am I okay? No, come to think of it, I'm not.

Because I've been knocked on my ass the last week since I learned that Halle now works for the Vikings. I'm seriously living in some kind of déjà vu Twilight Zone type of moment, and things keep getting stranger by the minute.

"Dane?" she asks again, concern in her voice. "Seriously, are you hurt?"

I chuckle. "Of course not. I'm fine. Pretty sure a kid her size can't do much damage to a guy my size. Although it was a close call."

Halle drops her hand, but the heat of her touch still lingers like a warm, pulsing glow over my skin.

"Good."

The girl, sandy-blond hair swinging like a pendulum behind her, is now bouncing on her toes, holding up some paper that appears to have been colored on. "Mama, Mama! Look, Mama! Look what I made for your new desk."

The word *Mama* doesn't quite register with me the first time it's spoken. Or the second. But by the third time, I realize it's directed at Halle.

I blink, my attention swinging back to Halle, and the

question flies out of my mouth.

"You have a kid?"

I sound like I've tasted something that doesn't agree with me, but I don't mean to. I'm just in disbelief over the idea that someone I once dated already has a kid.

I suppose Halle could be married by now. That thought gives me a sad pause.

My question—or the way it was asked—has Halle's cheeks turning impossibly red. *Cherry* red.

Her tongue sweeps out over her own heart-shaped lips, and her bright teal eyes meet my gaze head-on with a look of serious determination.

"Yes. This is my daughter, Lennon." She bends down and swoops her daughter into her arms, settling her onto her hip. "Lenni, this is Dane Axelrod. He's a Vikings hockey player, and they call him Ax. Say hello."

Lennon grows suddenly shy, winding her arms tightly around Halle's neck and burrowing her face into her mother's neck. A neck I've been intimately familiar with. I remember how warm and soft it was. The dainty curve of it that I traced with my tongue and kissed with my lips.

I give myself a mental shake. *Get your head in the game, bro.*

Lenni waves a hand that still clutches the drawing and murmurs, "Hi" from her position in Halle's embrace. Halle lifts her eyebrows as if to say *What can you do?* And then pries the paper from her daughter's hand so she can hold it out for inspection.

"My goodness. Lenni, this is so beautiful! Thank you. Do you want to tell Ax what you drew?"

She shakes her head timidly.

I tilt my head to the side, dropping my chin so I can peer into her face. "Do you mind if I take a look anyway?"

Her soft pewter eyes stare at me, and she gives a little nod of approval. Halle tips her head up to me, her mouth curving into an appreciative smile, and I take the paper from her fingers. A sizzle of electricity skirts up my arm the minute we touch, and I nearly snap my hand away, fumbling with the picture.

I look down at the handmade drawing. It appears to be a rendition of Lenin and her mom standing next to a house. In the top right corner are three tiny stick-figure people. There's also a black circle that looks like a hockey puck—definitely not drawn to scale—that's half the size of the house.

Surprisingly, the picture gives me a pretty good idea of what's going on in Halle and Lennon's lives. Or at least, I think I'm on the right track. I'm no kid-art expert.

I turn the picture around to face them and point to the icons. "This is a really good drawing. Is this you and your mommy and your new house?"

Lenni lifts her head and nods emphatically. I mean, I'm not too familiar with kids, but I have been known to charm a lot of women. I'm thinking same skills employed, just different audience.

"Mm-hmm."

Then I point to the people in the corner. "And who are these people?"

"That's my papa." She first points to the larger of the three stick figures and then extends her small hand to the guy now standing at my side. My gaze follows the direction she's pointing and I come face-to-face with Halle's dad. I remember meeting him a few times back in Calgary when Halle and I dated, but I can't for the life of me remember his name.

I give him a nod but don't say anything. Luckily, I have his granddaughter to help me out.

"And what's your papa's name?" I ask, deploying my stealthy spy skills.

She giggles, swinging her head first to Halle and then to her grandfather.

"*Papa*," she states with certainty, and gives me a critical look like I'm some kind of idiot. Fair point. Kids her age probably don't know first names of their immediate family members.

This earns chuckles from all of us, and I look like the fool she made me out to be.

I snicker. "Ahh, of course."

Halle's dad jumps in to save me from further embarrassment, giving me a clap on the back and extending his hand to shake mine. "Clint MacAlister. And it's good to see you again, Dane. We've watched your career grow over the years, and I'm proud to say I knew you when."

I peer at Halle and notice the red-tinged neck and

cheeks have returned once again. I raise an eyebrow at her, and she rolls her eyes.

Turning back to Clint, I shake his hand. "Good to see you again too, Clint. Are you still in Calgary? Or here permanently?"

"Nah. I've just been here to help my girls get settled. I'm leaving soon, but I'm looking forward to seeing you play tonight."

"Oh, yeah?" I pin Halle with my knowing gaze. "You're attending the game?"

Halle shrugs indifferently.

"I really wish the two boys could be here, too, but they're busy with school and their own hockey."

That's right. Halle had two younger brothers who both played hockey. Back when I was playing juniors, they were at the rink all the time, which is how Halle wound up working part time at the concession stand. Although she was their older sister, she'd been respon-sible for them after her mother died. That always impressed me about Halle. She was far more mature than any of the other girls I'd met.

My eyes travel back to Halle, who smooths her daugh-ter's hair away from her face. It's such a tender, motherly gesture that it warms the inside of my chest with its sweetness. I examine both of their faces. Lennon's coloring is somewhat different from Halle's, who has dark teal-blue eyes and reddish-brown hair. Their mouths are the same shape, though, and their button noses are very similar.

Lennon is an adorable girl with an infectious smile and laugh.

"How are your brothers doing?"

Halle looks first to Clint and then back to me, her expression turning to sisterly love.

"Good. Zack's playing college hockey in Utah, and Drew is a high school senior and playing juniors. Just like you did." Her bright blue eyes flash something I can't quite read, and she quickly turns away.

Is she thinking what I am? How she was adamant she didn't want anything to do with me because I was a *hockey boy*, as she called me? How I won her over, and we spent every moment we could in that short time we had that winter?

Does she remember how intense things were between us? How good they were? So good that she gave me her virginity?

I was such a dumbass for giving it all up and walking away from her.

A wave of regret washes over me. I clear my throat, now dry from the memories that haunt me and the awkwardness of this moment. It's one thing to have a run-in with an ex, but then to add her dad and her child, to boot? The longer I stay, the more likely I am to say something stupid. I need to get out of here.

"Well, hey, it was good to see you both again," I blurt out, reaching a hand to clap Clint on the back and turning toward Halle again. I don't know what I expected when I stopped down to say hello, but it sure wasn't this.

She's a mom. I itch to learn more about her life, but now isn't the time or the place.

"I'll see you around, Cherry. Maybe we can do lunch or coffee after practice someday soon. I'd love to properly catch up."

I'm about to place a kiss on Halle's cheek but stop myself, remembering where and who we are now.

Instead, I grin widely at Lennon and wiggle my fingers in front of her face. Then I bop the tip of her nose with a fingertip.

"Nice to meet you, too, Lulu Lennon. I hope you're coming to watch my game tonight too."

Her face contorts into a frown of protest. "My name's not *Lulu*. It's just Lenni."

I chuckle and give Halle one final glance before I head toward the elevators.

As I wait for the doors to open, I hear Lenni ask her mom a question, and I smile.

"Mama, why did Ax call you Cherry?"

8

____

Halle

I need a life-size facepalm emoji to use right now as I remain rooted utterly speechless after this unexpected run-in with Dane. I can feel the attention from both my dad and PJ on me.

My dad stares at me with an eyebrow quirked skyward, and I know exactly what he's thinking.

Hal, you need to tell Dane about his daughter.

This entire situation is a complete clusterfuck and unbelievably complicated. Dane just met his daughter for the first time and doesn't even know it.

Gah! I am an idiot for letting this happen.

Lenni wiggles in my arms. "Mama, let me down. I want to put your picture on your desk."

I absently do as my daughter requests and direct her to the cube next door while my dad introduces himself to PJ. They begin chatting about the recent preseason games and how the team looks for the year ahead. Even in my daze from the conversation with Dane, I can hear the level of unrestrained excitement my dad has over attending the game, and it makes me so happy that I can give him this opportunity.

As I help Lenni find the tape in my desk drawer, I mull over all the hundreds of possibilities I've rehearsed in my head about how I will someday explain to Dane that we made a child together.

But that someday isn't today. The timing has to be perfect. It's not every day you share such important news with the father of your child.

I've considered every option, including springing it on him when he's having one of the best days ever. Like, sharing it with him after he wins the Stanley Cup. He'd be on such a hockey-loving high that the idea of becoming an instant father wouldn't faze him.

I'd go up to him outside of the locker rooms, look him in the eye, and say, "Congratulations, Ax. You did it! You won the Cup! Oh, and by the way, you also have a daughter you never knew about! Isn't that great news? DING DING DING. You're the *big* winner!"

Corny and lame, I know. But how else do you go about breaking the news to your former boyfriend—I guess I can call him that—that he knocked you up five years ago and is now a father?

And then there's the tiny little issue that I've kept this news from him all this time. Since I have no clue how Dane may feel about the subject, I have to prepare for the various emotions that may arise. Anger. Confusion. Denial. And maybe even grief.

The best-case scenario? That Dane will be empathetic and understand the reasons why I chose to keep him in the dark after I learned I was pregnant and not to pursue any paternity rights.

My daughter's small grunt of exertion as she reaches her small arm across my desk to adhere the picture to the wall draws my attention back to the present. The paper is taped haphazardly and slants sideways. I leave it as is, her efforts making me smile with pride.

"Ahh, thanks, sweet pea. You're such a good artist and drew me such a beautiful picture. It will make me smile every time I look at it."

I stroke her soft cheek with my thumb and bend to kiss the top of her head once again, noticing the recent changes in her hair color. The light blond hair has begun to deepen into a darker shade of goldenrod. Just like her father's.

"Are you ready to go meet your new teacher?"

Lenni nods and squeals with excitement. "Yeeeees!"

I'm happy that she has this much enthusiasm over this new change. It means she's growing up and learning to accept new things and people without trying to hide. I put my finger to my lips to shush her. "Inside voice, please."

She giggles and jumps to the floor.

I've been so worried that this move would turn her world topsy-turvy. I'm taking her away from the only family she's ever known, and I think Dad's absence will be felt once he leaves.

I know I'll miss his daily presence and support.

Lenni grabs my hand, and we beckon my dad, who wraps up his conversation with PJ.

"Nice meeting you, PJ," he says, shaking his hand. "I appreciate you looking out for my daughter and teaching her the ropes."

"You bet, Clint." PJ's eyes dart to mine as I give him a curious stare. He nods. "It's great to have her here. And enjoy the game tonight."

My dad offers a broad smile. As he's been a lifelong hockey fan, I've never seen him happier than the day I told him I got the job with the Vikings. We knew it would be tough for me to move and branch out on my own. We had many late-night conversations about Lenni's needs and how I was going to manage it all by myself, hours away from my dad and brothers.

Although he's never outright broached the subject of Dane, Dad has made comments here and there about how he could have never managed to juggle all the balls with the family after my mom died without my assistance. Hidden within those comments was the fact that me being around meant he had help in raising my brothers. I was there to manage the household and care for my brothers when he was on long trips.

I understand his concerns. He's my dad and Lenni's grandfather. His job is to protect us and provide support. He's done that for years and I'll be eternally grateful. But now it's time for me to let go of that rope and learn to balance the life I've chosen to live on my own.

If millions of other single parents can do it, then so can I.

Starting with the incredible on-site daycare that the Vikings organization provides. My steps grow more confident as my dad and I walk side by side while Lenni races down the hall like a kid hopped up on candy and ice cream. Dad gives me a gentle bump of his shoulder against mine, and I heave out a heavy sigh, curling into the arm he wraps around my back and fitting my head in the crook of his elbow.

"You doing okay, Hal? I know this is a lot." He squeezes my arm lovingly. "I've been concerned it might prove too much for you and Len. But I'm so proud of you for taking on this challenge."

Emotion clogs my eyes and tears form at the corners of my eyes, and I give them a quick swipe with my finger. "Thanks, Dad."

"You know, I'm just an hour and a half plane ride away. And your aunt Marie is just down in Surrey if you run into any emergencies."

I know he's just trying to be helpful, but there is no reason I'd ever reach out to Aunt Marie. She was my mother's older sister by ten years, and they never had a close relationship. I think I may have seen her a total of three times during my childhood, and one of them was at my mom's funeral. Marie isn't the warm and friendly type. She was always too busy with work or travel to be bothered with family matters.

Perhaps I hold a grudge because of how cold and distant she was with my brothers and me at the funeral. She looked down at us with pity.

I tip my chin and give my dad a direct look. "Well, then, let's hope for our sakes there are no emergencies."

This garners a bark of laughter from my dad, and we round the corner toward the Little Vikings preschool and daycare.

Lenni—who is still five steps ahead of us—stands stock-still in the middle of the hallway, her back to us, like a boulder planted into a mountainside. Then she suddenly turns her face to look at us, her mouth gaping open. Her eyes light up in astonishment, and a giggle escapes her chest.

"Mama, Papa—look!" she exclaims with all the joy that can only emanate from a four-year-old. "It's a rainbow on the wall!"

She points to the long wall opposite the windowed room and jumps up and down. It indeed is a painted rainbow, bookended with white puffy clouds and birds flying on either side in the blue painted sky. She moves to the wall, jutting out her finger to touch each color in the mural.

"Wed, gween, blue," she says, all her Rs replaced with the W sound. She also has trouble pronouncing the *th* sound. But when I asked her pediatrician during her last checkup, the doctors said that's typical of young children and will resolve as she grows. Even now, I've noticed it sorting itself out.

"Good job knowing your colors," a female voice says from inside the room. We all turn to find a young woman, perhaps my age or a few years older, wearing a polka-dotted dress, jean jacket, and a pair of white sneakers, and smiling from the doorway. "You must be Lennon MacAlister."

Lenni hesitates and then rushes back to me, wrapping her arms around my leg like an octopus. She did the same thing a bit ago when she met Dane. But oddly, she warmed up almost immediately.

I extend my hand in greeting to the woman I believe is one of her new teachers. "Hi there. I'm Halle MacAlister and this is my father, Clint. And as you've determined, this is Lennon. Or Lenni."

We shake hands, and she kneels on the ground to greet Lenni at eye level.

"Hi there, Lenni. My name is Miss Adelaide. But you can call me Miss Addy." She smiles at Lenni, who peers out from behind my leg. "Would you like to come inside the classroom, and I'll show you around? There are still a few of the kids here waiting for their families to pick them up, and I know they're all excited to meet you."

Lenni glances up to me with a dubious look, and I give her a reassuring nod of approval. She slowly untethers herself from my leg as Miss Addy stands, then takes hold of Miss Addy's outstretched hand. Something unfurls inside my chest, loosening from the tight restriction I hadn't realized had been there for weeks.

Letting go of people in life is difficult. It's a hard life lesson we all have to learn and tests our resiliency to manage through change.

Just like letting go of my father's helping hand in order to learn how to become self-reliant. I know this is the boost Lenni and I both need to become independent women. Lucky for us, though, my dad will always be around to bail me out if I need his help.

I suppose it's part of the reason why I broke off the connection with Dane. At the time, I knew we both had to live our own lives and it would be best for both of us.

But this experience of watching Lenni leave me is an important life lesson for us both, too. Learning to fly even when we're not sure we're capable of doing it on our own.

I give her a wave, trying to keep my composure and the tears from spilling from the corners of my eyes. "Bye, sweet pea. I love you!" My voice cracks, and I point in the opposite direction. "I'll be just down the hall if you need me."

"Bye!" She waves and walks into the classroom. My dad squeezes my arm.

"You're doing great, Hal. You've got this."

Yeah, I've got this.

9

The game against Florida was tight the first two periods, and we are tied going into the third. Florida has ten more shots on goal than us, but thankfully Wolf has been an animal in the net, as his name implies. He's done one hell of a job stopping those fuckers from scoring.

I leave the ice after a shift and watch tonight's first line skate hard to make some plays and hold off the attacks of our worthy opponents. Right now, it's Costa, Canners, Lundy, Brewsky, and Thorny, our playmaker, out there, and they just got the rebound from a deflected shot.

Thorny grabs the puck and they fly down the ice toward the zone, Costa out in front where he receives a quick dish from Thorny. Canners swings around to the outside of the net as the puck gets passed between Lundy and Brewer. Then Costa pushes past his defender, grabs the puck and shoots, but it's deflected off Florida's goalie.

Fuck. It's so hard to watch from the bench, wishing I could be in there to help my teammates.

But with his catlike reflexes, Canners reaches out with his stick and catches the rebound, swinging around in front of the net, jamming his stick under the puck, and flipping the biscuit right over the goalie's shoulder to score.

"Fuck yeah!" I shout along with thousands of others in the arena. Canners bends a knee and raises his stick in the air in a celly. He skates along the boards in his victory dance as the lines quickly swap, and I'm jumping back out on the ice.

"Nice work, Canners," I congratulate him, giving him a fist bump on his way to the bench. A wide grin expands across his normally serious face. Brett has always been a closed-off kind of guy and rarely shows any emotion outside of frustration when he feels he doesn't contribute to the team.

Me? I'm the chatterbox of the team. Well, me and Rossy. Some guys leave it to the ice where they chirp nonstop, but Rossy and I bring it out all the time. The guys call it getting Axed, and bets have been placed on how long it might take for me to get to the end when I'm telling them a story or a joke.

Except I haven't shared with anyone that our new team analyst is my ex.

My thoughts go back to when I was leaving Ballas's

office earlier today. He'd called me down to talk about their decision to bring up a new kid from our AHL team and ask me to act as a mentor for him.

I admit, it felt pretty good to be tapped on the shoulder for something as important as that. I've always been a little bit on the cocky side. I mean, I was the highest scoring player my rookie season in the league. That means something.

But it's low-key cool to know Ballas sees me as an unofficial leader on the team, too. He has helped build my skills in that area and for that I'm grateful. He's taken me under his wing, given me some added responsibility, and guided me into becoming a mature player.

But that doesn't come close to the level of maturity that Halle must have had to become a mother at such a young age. It still blows my mind.

A mother.

For fuck's sake, that's taking responsibility to a whole other dimension. Halle is going on twenty-five, the same age as me, but she's a freaking *mom*. Holy shit. That really caught me off guard, just like that puck off the stick I took last season.

Something that feels like a scalding iron to my heart threatens to drop me to my knees when I consider that Halle could still be with Lenni's father.

The potential thought-spiral is interrupted when I hear my name being called. My head snaps in the direction of Wyatt, my line's left winger, who pushes the puck toward the zone and is looking for me to get positioned for a hand-off.

I deke the Florida defensive player, stealing past him to arc around the boards behind the net. Wyatt then dekes his opponent and slaps the puck toward me as I round the left of the goalie. Schmittie, a D-man, blocks the Florida guy, and with a flick of my wrist, I backhand the puck, sending it sailing past the goalie's outstretched leg and into the net.

Fuck yeah.

The buzzer horn blows to indicate the goal: my first goal of the game to go with my two assists from earlier. It brings us ahead by one, with under a minute of play remaining in regulation. I pump my fist in the air as my line surrounds me in a circle of celebration. Thumps of appreciation from the boys bump the top of my helmet.

The crowd is on their feet and going wild, the cheers and excitement filling the arena with a deafening noise. I shove my stick in the air over my head and take a celebratory lap, reveling in the smiles of the fans who beat on the glass as I pass them.

Just as I near the bench, I notice two blond pigtails with blue and orange ribbons—our team colors— swinging back and forth and bobbing up and down. I look more closely and see they belong to Lenni, who is being hoisted in the air by her grandfather.

In a spur-of-the-moment decision, I whip off one of my gloves and glide to a stop in front of the glass. I tap on it and point and wave at her. Lenni smiles shyly and waves, dropping her eyes to Clint for assurance. He smiles and nods at me, then my gaze travels to Halle, who stands next to him and is wearing a Vikings jersey and clapping along in celebration.

Our eyes meet for less than two seconds.

But in those two seconds of time, my breath is stolen from my lungs, and my heart skips a beat.

It doesn't matter that the entire arena screams *Ax! Ax! Ax!*

Or that my teammates are racing to join in my celebration.

All that matters in this moment is that I'm going to make a second chance to be with Halle happen. No matter what it takes.

There is a reason Halle is back in my life, and I will not waste one second of this opportunity. Logically, I know I have to find out about her relationship status. And even if she's single, it's impossible for us to go back to the beginning. But that doesn't mean I can't find a way to forge something new between us.

Before I skate back to my spot on the bench, I catch Halle's eye and motion with my glove, pointing first to my eyes and then to her.

And then I wink.

10

————

Halle

With my dad zonked out and fast asleep on the living couch and Lenni asleep in her own bedroom, I have a quiet moment to call my best friend, Carmen, and tell her all that's happened in the last week. Especially what transpired today in my office and at the arena tonight.

"Oh my God, Carmy. The way he looked at me, though... and that wink... I don't know what that was about, but it was intense."

Carmy snorts loudly and rolls her eyes at me. I swear, she always wants to video chat just so she can practice that obnoxious move.

"Girl, what I saw in that *Sports Night* replay clip was flat-out eye-fucking. *Holy shit*. The entire sports world got an eyeful of that, honey." She fans herself with her notebook as she walks down the street toward her apartment in Edmonton.

Carmy is my oldest and closest friend. We have known each other since childhood, and she was there every step of the way when I learned I was pregnant with Lennon. The tough part is the huge distance we face now that I'm in BC and she's attending law school at the University of Alberta. Carmy is the closest thing to an auntie that Lennon has had, and she misses her desperately. So do I.

Carmy is also well aware of my previous relationship with Dane since she was around that winter, and she understands the reasons I have chosen to withhold the information about Lenni's paternity.

Although she initially pressed me to contact Dane to tell him about Lenni, she never judged me for deciding not to.

She didn't agree with it, but she respected my right to protect my daughter.

Or was it myself that I had been protecting?

All the lines have become blurry now that Dane and I have run into each other and he's met Lenni.

"I think he hates me." I turn away from the screen and say the words in barely a whisper.

Carmen obviously heard it because she tilts her head to the side and gives me that judgey look of hers, her dark eyes glaring into the camera.

"Hate you?" she scoffs, squinting as if the sun's too bright, even though she's now inside. "Hal, I'm not sure what erroneous narrative you're telling yourself, but my vast legal training tells me that that man has some very big unresolved feelings for you, and hate is definitely not one of them."

I stare down at my hands in my lap, picking at one of my nails that Lenni valiantly and with the precision of a four-year-old repainted pink tonight. The polish is messy and clumpy, chipping off around the cuticles already. But I wouldn't trade the experience for the world.

My little girl loves to play dress-up and salon with me and anyone else who will be patient enough to let her. I think she inherited those genes from my mom, who would probably have her own *YouTube* channel dedicated to beauty tips and product use if she were still alive.

Those interests, sadly, apparently skipped a generation. The most makeup I've ever used on the regular is mascara, when I remember to put some on, and a lip balm to keep my lips from cracking in the middle of Calgary winters.

I remember the breakfast Dane and I had many years ago when I was dumbfounded why he would pursue me over all the other girls who would've killed to go out with him.

We had been in a booth at Smitty's eating breakfast after he practically hijacked me in my car after his morning practice and I'd asked him outright, "Why me?"

I wasn't looking to date anyone at the time, especially not a hockey boy. Two weeks after the Christmas and Boxing Day holidays, I was setting off to Montana State for my first semester of college. I'd delayed my start to earn some more money and take care of my brothers while my dad was on the road, but it was my turn. I didn't have time to date, and I didn't want to leave yet another person behind when I left for the States.

That day, Dane proved to me in words and deeds that he was a stand-up guy. Sure, he was extremely full of himself, arrogant beyond belief, but he was also charming and sweet. And he saw something in me that, honestly, I had never seen myself.

His response was a simple statement. He said, "You have something the other girls don't have."

That's all it took to hook me. After that, we began our month-long romance that was the closest thing I've ever had to a relationship. Since then, I haven't had time or the inclination to date anyone, and now I have Lenni to consider.

Carmen brings me back to the present with her next question.

"What are you going to do about him, Hal?"

I adjust myself against the pillows of my bed in my small yet functional bedroom. I've yet to unpack any of my things beyond some of the clothes that hang in the closet. My room can wait for me to organize. It was the kitchen and Lenni's things that were my priority. I wanted to make her feel at home as quickly as possible because I knew it would be a difficult transition once my dad left. At least, I think it will be, and I'm planning for the worst, hoping for the best.

Maybe I'm projecting my own fears and anxieties about life on her.

I sigh and wrinkle my brow. "I honestly don't know. I'm struggling to figure out what the right thing to do is in this situation. It's so freaking complicated."

"Yeah. Adulting sucks." She sticks out her tongue, and I laugh.

Carmen always knows how to cheer me up and put me in a better headspace. I guess that's what friends are for. She would've been here to help me with the move, but she's right in the middle of exams and couldn't take the time away, which is exactly as it should be. I'm proud of her for the effort she's given to pushing through this tough second year of law school.

"How's school going?" I ask, realizing we've spent all this time talking about my problems and I haven't asked her about her life. "Oh, and how's Vincent?"

Vincent is her boyfriend, even though she says they aren't "labeling things"—unless it's when she's calling him her fuck toy.

She hoists a coffee mug in front of the camera and takes a drink, shooting me a wink. She always wears a wicked little gleam in her eyes.

"I'm drinking coffee at eleven o'clock on a Friday night. The fuck toy has already come—literally—and gone, and that should be some indicator how the rest of my night is going to go."

I chuckle. "So, your boyfriend isn't spending the night?"

"Pshh... not a chance. I told him the first time we fucked in the back of the library that he was never going to sleep in my bed. I have no room for that in my life. Only his dick. Coffee and his dick. That's all I need." She gives me a broad smile.

"How about a shot of Canadian whiskey? You got room for that in your coffee?"

"Good point. But I think I'm out. It's been a while since I've seen a grocery store. I better go check." She makes a face and takes another swig, setting the cup down somewhere in front of her on her desk. Then she stands up from her chair and walks into the tiny kitchen in her studio apartment on campus. She adjusts the phone so I can get a glimpse of the countertop, where she plucks the top off a bottle of wine instead and takes a swig right from the bottle.

"Ahh," she says, followed by a belch that would rival ones from my younger brothers. Recapping the bottle, she looks back at me in the camera. "Not hard liquor, but it will do. Ya know, five years ago, we would've been together, getting fucked up and laid at a party. Now look at us. We're both boring and sober and home by eleven."

I laugh. "*Riiight.* You are never boring, my friend. And I was the good girl back then if you recall." I hold my hand up under my chin and bat my eyelashes like some naïve child.

It is the truth. Carmy was always the more rebellious and adventurous of us. I was far less into parties and guys and more into studying. I had the responsibilities of taking care of Zack and Drew, and I wanted the scholar-ship advantages that good grades could get me. Carmen came from money and knew she'd get to where she was going regardless of her social life in high school.

I never had the time to indulge, and nothing much has changed except that I'm now in a different city and in my own place.

She laughs loudly and then *tsks* with a wagging finger at the screen. "Innocent, my ass. Remember, girlfriend, I know exactly what happened in my guest room the night of my holiday party."

I can't help it, I blush. It's ridiculous to be embar-rassed over that rite of passage, the night I slept with Dane and lost my virginity.

That was the night I fell for a hockey player, and it changed my life.

11

———

H alle – Five Years Earlier

I need to leave. I need to get dressed and get out of here before I do something stupid.

Like fall for this hot hockey-playing boy.

But I can't seem to move my feet. I lean over the side of the bed and grab for my sweater, shoving it through my arms and over my head before I make the mistake of looking back at Dane's naked body.

It's a glorious work of art. I stare at his impressive semi-hard length, salivating for the missed opportunity of tasting him on my tongue tonight. I sigh and, snapping back around, root around in search of my panties.

That's when one muscled arm shoots out and secures me around my middle, tugging me back so I fall sideways against the mattress.

"Where are you going, Cherry? We have all night."

I shake my head and try to push myself back up, but he squeezes me tighter, fingers splayed across my belly.

"I can't... I've got to leave." The words sound unconvincing even to my own ears.

Dane ignores my response. Instead, he nuzzles his mouth at my neck, his tongue drawing a wet path over the sensitive flesh there. I shiver at the touch, the sensation zinging down my spine and between my legs.

I can't control the moan that escapes my mouth, and Dane chuckles low against my ear.

"Mm-hmm. That's what I thought."

Dane's hand slides underneath my sweater and up my belly. His featherlight touch skims over my stomach and ribs, and then over the cup of my lacy bralette. I rarely wear anything but sports bras, but tonight I had wanted to feel sexy. And it had worked.

When his thumb circles my pebbled nipple, I ball the sheet in my fist, and that same needy moan tumbles past my parted lips. Wetness pools between my legs now, and an emptiness in my core demands to be rectified. It becomes a need I can barely contain.

My breath accelerates as he continues to circle and cup the swells of my breasts, his own moans becoming choppy and breathy. His now fully hard erection pokes hungrily at me from behind. I have an urgent desire to touch him, to feel his hardness in my hand, in my mouth.

While he continues to play with my nipples, I snake my hand over my hip and behind me, reaching for his dick. When I curl my fingers around his taut, smooth skin and grip tight, a guttural groan surfaces from Dane's chest. His breath fans across my hair and his response makes me grin proudly. Slowly, I begin to stroke him in my hand, experimenting with the tempo and pressure, loving the weight of his girth in my palm.

Feeling braver with each moan he releases, I flip around to face him. Those steel-gray eyes are darker than I've seen them. I break our connection and glance down at his cock bobbing needily between his legs and drop my hand. He lets out a growl of disapproval.

Then I scoot down on my knees. There are blankets and sheets strewn around us to navigate but then I'm right where I want to be. My face hovers over his bare stomach, which ripples as it flexes. I find a light brown smattering of hair trailing from his belly button down to his groin and tentatively run the end of my fingertip along the path, then dip my tongue to follow that same trail.

I inhale the woodsy, musky scent of his body. Something inside me ignites from anticipation, my own need pulsing wildly at my core with every inch that my mouth gets closer to his straining erection.

Encircling him in my palm, I dip my head and swirl the tip of my tongue around the top of his crown. The action provokes a long, drawn-out groan from Dane's lips.

"Ah, fuuuuck, Cherry."

The honesty in his desire gives me the courage to continue my exploration of his insanely hot body. Centering myself between his open legs, my palms sweep along the inside of his *thighs before I position his crown against my lips and then slowly draw him into my mouth.*

The sound he makes is desperate, one that pleads for me to let him out of his misery.

I'm not sure what I'm doing or what to expect, but it's not the salty taste of him or how wide I must stretch my lips to fit around his girth. Regardless of my inexperience, I must be doing it right because Dane's whole body tightens and he exhales a shaky hiss of breath.

It emboldens me, and without any of the awkward hesitation from earlier, I give myself permission to suck him in and out of my mouth with fervor. I may not do it with finesse, but as I draw him in and take him to the back of my throat, I feel his thickness swell impossibly more. I peer up at him through my lashes and see his abs ripple when he props himself up on his elbows. His gaze is almost pained when he reaches out and threads his fingers through my hair.

"You better stop now, Cherry, or things are going to get messy."

I smile bashfully around his cock and swallow. He lets out a deep, shuttering breath.

"Ah, shit... yeah, I can't..." He flops back against the pillow, nostrils flaring, and his grip tightens on my head. "I'm too close, Cherry. I'm gonna come."

I'm painfully aware just how wet I am right now and the growing intensity of the throbbing presence between my legs. I know I'm in need of my own release but ignore it in favor of giving all my attention to Dane's hard cock.

I hollow out my cheeks and suck him further back until

he's hitting the back of my throat. I swallow around his girth as I feel his legs tighten and abs contracting as the first wave of his release hits my mouth.

My eyes flutter open in panic. I breathe in deeply through my nose, my throat muscles working furiously to keep up with all he's giving me. I taste his salty, earthy essence against my tongue, and it gives me a craving so strong I'm nearly blinded by it.

After Dane's body has relaxed and he pants in exhaustion, I pull my mouth free and sit back on my heels. I'm still in my bra and sweater, but my legs are bare and my panties are somewhere on the floor. The slickness between my legs is apparent, and the way Dane stares at me with hunger sends a thrill down my spine. The growing ache inside me intensifies.

He props himself up on one elbow, his bicep flaunting with the flex of his muscle as a slow, satisfied smile stretches across his face.

"Well, that takes care of one of us, eh?"

He says nothing more as he pushes himself to his knees, completely unfazed over his state of nakedness. Like a jungle cat, he inches closer, and I tug at the hem of my sweater, nervously trying to pull it down to cover the clear evidence of my arousal.

But he pushes my hand to the side and wedges his fingers inside the gap in my thighs, the rough pads of his fingertips toying with my sensitive skin.

"Still need to leave?"

Dane's dark eyes narrow on me, a knowing smile across his lips, and then his eyes drift down to where his hand rests. A nervous gasp escapes my mouth, and I bite the corner of my bottom lip, fighting back a lusty moan when he drags his fingers up the inside of my thigh.

I close my eyes and yield to his ministrations as his fingers search and find the wetness pooled along my skin. When his fingers part my slick folds, I collapse backward, knees pressing out as he begins to explore.

"Come here," he instructs, pulling on one hand so I rise on my knees. "Put your hands on my shoulders. You're gonna want to hold on."

I lift my arms and wrap my hands behind his head, my fingertips grazing the soft hair at his nape.

The moment my hands lock together, his thumb slides deliciously through my wetness, circling my clit in a rhythm meant to send me flying to the moon.

My hips buck and grind madly into his hand, my body seeking friction by pressing into his palm. His chuckle is like warm liquid against my neck. A finger curls inside, then another, as they slide in and out of my body, which acts of its own accord.

I have a need to reach something I can't define. Something big and out of this world. The sensation is overwhelming and so strong, like a riptide taking me out to sea, swirling and tossing me from side to side, sending me in a dizzying direction.

I dig my fingers into the back of his shoulder blades and score my nails over the taut skin, bringing my mouth against the front of his collarbone to bite down into his hot flesh as an orgasm the size of a hurricane rips through me.

I cry out, muffling the husky sound against his neck. As

the pleasure subsides, the white stars behind my eyelids flickering out, I slump against his heated body. Dane's arm snakes around my waist and carefully brings us back onto the mattress so he can spoon me as I languidly enjoy the afterglow.

It could be mere minutes or hours, but however long it is, the sensation created by him spooning me is as close to heaven as I've ever been. It's like magic to be wrapped up in Dane's arms.

"I don't ever want to go," I whisper so quietly that I don't think he can hear me. Based on his response, though, he clearly does.

"I don't want that either." He places a kiss along the back of my neck. "Let's stay this way forever and never let each other go."

12

D ane
Not so long ago, I'd normally go out with the boys and celebrate the win or commiserate the loss with drinks and women.

The likelihood that I wouldn't crawl into bed before two a.m. had been relatively high. Usually, I'd hit the hay with a satisfied dick and a good buzz, falling into a sound sleep until morning.

But that routine, however, was blown to bits when Halle arrived on the scene, followed by the strange and electric moment I shared with her tonight. Those sapphire teal eyes of hers have left me wide awake at 3 a.m., trying to rid her from my thoughts.

I'm not sure I've ever felt anything as powerful as I did the moment I noticed Halle watching me from the stands. It threw me and the rest of my night into a wild tailspin. I've been a fucking mess, a literal buzzkill as I hang with Costa, Rossco, and the rookies. I had one beer and am calling it a night, much to Rossco's dismay.

"You're being a weenis," Rossco whines when I say I'm leaving. "A weenis who's not going to get laid by leaving."

He's right. If I stay, I'd likely get a good buzz on and maybe find a gorgeous woman to hookup with. But that's not my vibe and not what I'm looking for tonight. I don't want anyone else besides Halle. And I don't want to forget about the fire that was reignited in my soul when her gaze tangled with mine. The memories that it's evoked has my headspace cluttered and in turbulent chaos.

All I know is I'm on a mission to find out if she's with someone else. And if not, to get back in her life.

Now, after leaving the bar to boos and hisses from the boys, I stare up at the living room ceiling of my condo and contemplate the one true regret of my life. What would our lives be now if we hadn't ended things that winter? Would she have ended up married to someone else with a kid?

Although, now that I think about it, she wasn't with a guy tonight other than her dad, no sign of anyone else around. Why would her dad be here helping with Lennon and the move instead of a partner?

I'm probably overlooking a thousand possibilities. Maybe she's with someone who travels for work and is out of town at the moment. I remember that Clint was a long-haul trucker, which was the reason Halle took care of her brothers in his absence.

Thoughts swirl in my mind as I slide a hand behind my head and stretch my legs down the length of the couch. There's also another possibility to consider.

What if Halle and her daughter's father didn't work out? That could explain the absence of a husband or partner.

A slow smile draws across my mouth at the thought that Halle could be single.

I let out a long sigh, clasping both hands together behind my head, then close my eyes and let memories wash over me like a cascading waterfall, drenching me with images of our short time together.

The time I spent with Halle, albeit brief, had been the best time of my life. We were on the cusp of adulthood and hanging on to our teens but looking forward to the future. Being with Halle made me realize there was more to life than just hockey. There was something bigger to chase and hold on to.

But I didn't hold on to her.

At the time, what we had together seemed important, seemed like something that could stand the test of time. But then she said goodbye and I agreed it was for the best.

I should've fought harder for her. I shouldn't have given up so easily.

Honestly, it's pathetic to think about, but it hurt my ego that she didn't want to continue the relationship. So instead of fighting for what I wanted, I tucked those true feelings away. I didn't want to look like some lovesick schmuck. I wasn't going to beg her to stay with me.

That night, I acted like losing her was no big thing.

"Dane... I think we need to say goodbye." She pauses, *chewing on her lip. "So, you know, let's just part as friends."*

I stare up at this beautiful girl and know I will never find another quite like Halle.

"Just promise that you won't forget me, Dane."

"Never," I whisper. "I will never forget you, Cherry. I promise."

I never did forget about her, but losing her cost me.

It cost me time with her. And in the process, I closed off my heart and never allowed another woman in.

Now that I have a chance to reflect, I see that Halle has always been in the recesses of my mind. Whenever I was alone or something jogged my memory, she was right there.

From the moment I saw her with cherry slushie dripping down her face and over her clothes, I knew she was still the most beautiful girl I'd ever seen.

Uncharacteristic of me at the time, I chased her down and took her to breakfast the next time I saw her. From that moment on, it was impossible to resist the pull she had me.

After our first night together, we worked hard to carve out time to see each other and find places where we could hang out in private. Creativity was the name of the game back then when neither of us had privacy in our homes. I was living with a hockey billet family in

Calgary, and her dad was taking time off the road for the holidays, which made it difficult to locate spots where we could get naked and fuck each other's brains out.

But as the saying goes, *if there's a will, there's a way,* and we found ways.

Me: Hey, I'm outside.

Cherry: Outside where?

Me: Your house. Come to the window. Hurry. I'm freezing my ass off.

My entire body is numb as I stand outside of Halle's house. I snuck out of my host family's house tonight, walked a mile in the freezing cold and snow, and now wait below Halle's second-floor bedroom window.

"What are you doing here?" Halle asks through the open window. She wraps her arms around her flannel pajama-covered body, her sleepy smile enough to get me hard, and steps to one side.

I carefully hoist myself through the window frame and toe off my snowy boots as she closes the window behind me. When I turn around, she is standing inches from me, and I can feel the warmth of her body in the small space between us.

"I told you I wanted to see you."

I remove my team jacket and hat, tossing them on the floor, and take a step toward her. Closing the distance, I wrap my arms around her back, my hands landing in the slight curve above her ass. I stare down into her eyes, and she loops her hands behind my neck.

I raise an eyebrow. "Here I am."

She giggles. "Here you are, and you're freezing."

Her hands move to cup my face in her palms. I plant my lips on hers. They are warm and wet, and I missed her taste.

"So warm me up."

I position one hand on her hip and slip the other underneath the waistband of her pajama bottoms. Sliding it toward her bottom, I cup the round globe of her butt, squeezing the soft flesh. Halle moans into my mouth. My tongue makes a hot, wet sweep inside as I seek pleasure and surrender to the primal need of kissing her.

Before I lose all control, I drag my mouth from hers and give her a meaningful—hopeful—look.

"Are you okay that I'm here? We don't have to do anything if you—"

My words are hijacked when she snags my wrist and tugs me to the bed, giving me a push against my chest so I fall backward across her mattress.

"Shut up, Hockey Boy," she says, her eyes flashing with heat. She reaches confidently to the buttons of my jeans, undoing them and dragging the cold denim down my legs so I can kick them off my feet.

Repositioning herself above me, she slowly undoes the buttons of her Christmas-tree pajama top, opening the flannel material so her breasts are exposed for my viewing pleasure.

I swallow thickly when she wiggles free of her bottoms and is left fully naked on top of me.

Her nipples pucker, and I reach out my hand to graze a stiff peak with the pad of my thumb.

"You look cold, Cherry. Maybe you need to be warmed up." I lift my head and flick her distended nipple with the tip of my tongue before curling my lips over the peak and sucking hard.

Halle gasps loudly, and I rear back, eyes darting toward the bedroom door, where I notice the sliver of light illuminating the crack at its base.

"It's okay," she encourages, reaching for the hem of my Henley and tugging it over my head. "My brothers are playing video games in the basement, and my dad is asleep with his CPAP machine. They won't hear a thing."

"Good, because I'm going to make you scream so loud the windows will shatter."

She giggles. "Are ya now, eh?"

I loop my arm around her waist and flip her onto her back, wedging my leg between her thighs. Oh Christ, she's so hot. Her naked body is all heat and silk, and I want to bury myself inside her and let her fire consume me.

Our mouths collide, our hands exploring every inch of each other's skin and bodies until we're both panting and in need of release.

Suddenly I realize there's no one else I want to be with. I know the clock is ticking, but I don't want to rush things. Everything about her is perfect, and I want this moment with her tonight to last.

I remove the condom stashed in my jeans pocket and fit it over my erection, then position myself at her entrance. As I slowly edge the tip of my cock inside her slippery, aroused flesh, I stare down at Halle, her wavy hair spread over the pillow, eyes filled with anticipation and naked desire.

I reach down and sweep my thumb over her cheek, cupping her jaw before I lean down and—

I jerk upright on the couch, the haze of sleep and the dream lost as I come fully awake. I'm hit with an image that has me agitated and vibrating with tension.

It's of a little girl with soft-gray eyes, blonde hair, and a smile that brings out a cute indentation in the middle of her chin.

Halle's daughter, Lennon.

What the fuck?

I scrub a hand over my head, trying to dislodge the question that's been bouncing back and forth since the day I met Lennon.

It's not possible. No fucking way.

Or is it?

Am I Lennon's father?

13

———

H alle
After sending my dad off this morning with lots of waves goodbye and the sad whimpering tears from one very unhappy granddaughter, Lenni and I kept busy the rest of the day getting some chores done and exploring Vancouver.

Since we've been having gorgeous fall weather, we decided to check out Stanley Park. Lenni especially loved the rose gardens and walking along the Seawall, where people biked, walked, and ran around the waterfront. It was a new experience for both of us to smell the briny scent of the English Bay in the air and listen to the squawk of seagulls as they flew overhead before diving into the lapping waves to catch their food.

Bedtime came too fast by Lenni's estimation. While she takes her evening bath, I sit perched on the edge of the old porcelain tub and watch her play with the new rubber sea lion we picked up at one of the souvenir shops.

"Mama, where do baby sea lions come from?" she asks thoughtfully, dipping the toy underneath the waterline and then letting it go to pop back up to the surface.

"From their mommies' tummies, just like human babies."

She turns her attention to me, water dripping down the side of her cheek. I reach over and catch the water droplet with my fingers.

"Is that where I came from? Your tummy?"

I nod. "Yep. You were right in here." I rub my lower stomach, which had been distended to the size of a basketball while I was pregnant with her.

Lenni squints in concentration. "How did I get out?"

I consider my response, not wanting to go too far in the details and end up freaking her out. These types of things can be a bit traumatizing for little kids, not to mention adding a string of questions sure to follow.

"Well, when a baby is ready to be born, a mommy goes into what's called labor and has to go to the hospital."

Lenni's mouth puckers in an *O*. She lifts the bath toy in the air and examines it, flipping it over in her slick hands. I'm waiting for her follow-up question when my phone pings with a message notification.

It's probably either my dad or Carm with their daily

check-in. I reach toward where it sits on the top of the bathroom vanity, where I had put it earlier so it'd be out of the way of any splashing water.

But the phone nearly slips from my fingers when I see who it's from. I blink down at the contact name on the display.

Hockey Boy.

Son of a biscuit. That's not who I thought I'd get a message from tonight.

What the hell does he want?

Nope.

I don't care.

I set the phone back down on the edge of the counter and peer at Lenni to make sure she's okay, my head whirling over what Dane could possibly want with me.

My curiosity gets the best of me, and I know it will eat away at me if I don't read that text this instant. I grab the phone again and tap the message box displaying his name, tentatively scanning it like it's a snake ready to strike.

Although I had blocked his number for self-preservation after he was drafted, hoping it would save me from any pregnancy hormone slip-ups, I had unblocked it when Lenni was about two. At the time, she'd fallen and we thought she had a broken arm. When we went to the hospital, I was concerned I might need to know her father's blood type, which meant I'd have to reach out to him.

Now as I stare at the phone and message, I wonder if I should've blocked it again.

> Hockey Boy: Hey Cherry. Is this still your number?

Lenni splashes in the water, and some of it sluices over the edge, hitting my bare feet. At the shock of both the water and the surprise text, I screech out in surprise, my attention drawn away from the additional texts that I hear ping, one after the other. I put the phone back on the counter's edge.

"Are you okay, Mama?" Lenni asks worriedly. I raise my eyes and give her a gentle smile.

"I'm fine, sweet pea. The water was just cold on my foot." I lean down and dab at the droplets with the orange duck-hooded towel, replacing it on the hook on the wall when I'm done. "Ten more minutes, my little duckie."

She giggles at this. "Mama, I'm a baby seal tonight."

"Oops, that's right. I forgot. You do look like a little sea lion." I give her wet nose a bop with my fingertip, and she giggles some more. "Do you remember what the sign we read today said about sea lions?"

Lenni's forehead wrinkles and furrows in concentration. We'd stopped at every sign along the path, and I'd read aloud each one, educating us both on the various lives of marine life in the bay.

She holds up the rubber seal toward me, wiggling it in her now pruning fingers. "They aren't fish, but I don't 'member what they are." Her lips form into a pout.

"That's right. They aren't fish. They're called mammals. They're warm-blooded, just like you and me. Fish are cold-blooded. And, because they're mammals, they don't lay eggs like fish do. They have babies."

She grins, showing off a dimpled chin that immediately conjures Dane's image in my mind and has me itching to read the other texts that came in.

Instead, I focus on Lenni. My priority.

"Just like you had me at the *hospital*?" she asks.

I nod. Most of the information I share may be too much for a four-year-old, but anytime I have the chance to provide her with educational lessons, I do. The more I can expose her to tidbits about life, the smarter she'll become. Which is why I read to her every night, and we watch YouTube videos and get Google to answer when she asks questions that I can't.

It's sometimes daunting the sheer number of questions that float around that tiny head of hers. I often wonder what parents did before the internet came along. Did they have to carry around an encyclopedia everywhere they went to feed their child's hungry brain?

And I can never get away with admitting I don't have the answer. Lenni will simply push until she's satisfied she understands. When I try saying, "I'm not sure, baby. I don't know," her immediate retort is, "Yes you do, Mama."

She thinks I'm a quiz-show contestant with all the answers.

Don't I wish.

The scariest question that she's yet to ask—though I

know it's coming at some point—is, "Why don't I have a daddy?"

As if right on cue, my phone pings again.

I swallow down the hard lump in my throat and shift my body away from Lenni, my knees bumping into the cabinet door of the vanity. I let out a grumbled curse under my breath and pick up the phone, using my body to covertly read the messages.

It's ridiculous that I'm hiding the screen, considering she can't read yet. But the secrecy involved with who it's from instinctively has my body shielding to protect my daughter from the implications of the texts.

Taking a deep breath and allowing the sweet song about sunshine that Lenni sings calm my nerves, I look down at the phone and read through the three back-to-back texts Dane just sent me.

Hockey Boy: If this is still you...

Hockey Boy: I need to talk to you about something important.

Hockey Boy: And I need you to be honest with me.

It appears there's a fourth coming, but right now it's just ellipses on my screen. I try to look away— hoping to avoid what is surely coming. The question that has been left unanswered for over five years now.

The answer to which I never thought I'd have to explain.

My palms sweat, my breathing accelerates, and my eyes prickle with unshed tears that are likely to pour out.

This is the moment of truth. The moment I've been dreading and avoiding yet also quietly waiting for all these years.

The issue remains that I still don't know if I want Lennon to find out who her father is.

It's not that I don't think she deserves the truth. It's that I'm not certain if Dane deserves her, which sounds so cruel to say.

Dane has never been a bad guy.

In fact, he was always incredibly sweet to me. He was extremely considerate during my first time. He was patient and thoughtful. He wooed me with his charm and charisma. Dane probably would've made a good boyfriend.

The problem is his profession and his ability to stick around for Lenni. The demanding job of a professional hockey player creates issues around stability and doesn't really support healthy relationships. How can it when players are on the road more than nine months out of every year?

I experienced that as a kid with my own father, who was rarely at home. It was my mom who kept our family together, and after she died, that responsibility fell to me.

I've never wanted that for my daughter. It's not fair to Lennon or, frankly, to me.

I blink down at the screen, noticing it shake in my

hand. My stomach is in knots and the pizza we ate for dinner is threatening to come back up.

I'm scared to read his next words.

I'm terrified of the consequences that the truth will create in our lives.

The text finally appears, and I want to climb into my bed and bury my head under the covers, ignore his question like it's a pile of dirty laundry.

Hockey Boy: Is Lennon my daughter?

I stare down at those four words for what feels like forever, lost in the situation that has finally been realized and come to light. The fork in the road that clearly delineates a turning point in our lives.

It shouldn't come as a surprise that he's figured it out. It doesn't take a detective to see they share a similarity in features and must be related in some way or another. Although I've never seen baby photos from Dane's childhood, I'd venture to guess Lenni is a mirror image of him at this age.

How do I respond and begin this conversation that will inevitably change all our lives?

I flick my gaze over my shoulder and watch Lenni, who is now sitting with her knees bent, her toy perched at the top of her skinny legs as she makes it swan-dive into the water below.

My heart clenches at the realization that whatever I say, there will be consequences. Consequences that will be everlasting and change the course of Lenni's life forever.

I lean over and place a kiss on top of her wet head, breathing in the sweet scent of baby shampoo, seeking some kind of solace before I open up Pandora's box.

And then I type out my response.

14

D ane

"Bruh, what's up with you today?"

I sit up from the workout bench, where I've just done an exhausting set of chest presses, and reach for my plastic water bottle, squirting some in my mouth. Costa, who is my spotter today, grabs the bottle from my hand and douses me with a deluge across my pecs.

"Fuck me, what's that for, you douche?" I wipe the mess away with the towel that's slung around my neck and give him a dirty look.

With our stretch of games at home this week, today is a strength and conditioning day. The next game is coming up on Thursday night.

"You're acting weird lately," he observes—rather correctly—nudging my head with his fist. "Weirder than usual. And if I didn't know how careful you are when you hook up, I'd think maybe you'd just learned you knocked somebody up."

I start coughing and sputtering wildly, the water I just sucked down spilling from the corners of my mouth and dribbling down my chin.

Jesus, is he a mind reader? Are my thoughts written all over my face?

Although technically, I'm still in the dark on the whole situation. Halle's response had been vague. The only thing I know with absolute certainty is that she will give me the story when we meet up at lunch today.

> Cherry: Yes, we should chat. But not now.

> Cherry: Lunch tomorrow. Meet me at the Ale House. 12:30 p.m.

I don't know what I expected when I so blatantly asked if I'm Lennon's dad in a text. It wasn't exactly the most tactful approach to pose the question. I suppose, if I put myself in her shoes, answering yes or no right then wasn't really an option. I'm sure there's more to the story and I do feel bad for putting her on the spot like that.

But it was driving me batshit crazy wondering if I somehow got Halle pregnant five years ago.

We were careful during sex. I knew back then I didn't want to have a kid when I was so young myself. I had too much going for me to have that additional responsibility. And like Costa said, I've always been vigilant with protection when hooking up.

I've made sure to wrap that shit up tight to protect everyone involved.

My dad had drilled it into me during the sex talk when I was thirteen and again before I went off to juniors when he said that sex was fun and a part of life, but there should always be safety first. And I was to always, without fail, be attentive to the needs of my partner and treat her with respect. I took those words to heart.

I've second-guessed myself a thousand times today, wondering if I'm seeing things that aren't there. Sure, Lennon has similar features to me, but that could just be a coincidence. And I did the math. Even if the last time Halle and I slept together was five years ago and Lenni happened after that, it's reasonable to assume Halle may have hooked up with some guy in college her first semester and, BAM, Lennon happened.

It doesn't mean she's my kid.

But what if she is?

My stomach clenches with something akin to fear. Not because I might find out she is my daughter, but the possibility that Lennon *isn't* mine. Something unfurls from deep within me that wants it to be true.

The thought baffles me, though, because I've never had any interest in being a dad. And once Halle left my life, I wasn't interested in having a committed relationship with anyone else, for that matter. None of it has been on my radar. My entire life and focus have always been on hockey and enjoying the privileges that come along with the lifestyle of being a player.

I'm brought back to the present by Costa's hand flapping in front of my face for my attention.

"Yo, Earth to Ax. Did you hear me?"

I blink up and he's looking back at me like I've grown two heads. "Yeah, yeah. I'm good. You want a spot?"

I stand up and use my towel to wipe off the sweat left behind, then gesture toward the bench.

He takes the seat but doesn't immediately lie down. Instead, he runs a hand through his tousled brown hair.

"Sommer's going to be here this week."

Now I'm just confused.

"Summer? It's fall, dude."

Costa pushes his palm against my hip. "Fucking hell, you really are out of it. Sommer is my *wife*, bruh."

Oh, yeah, his wife. The one he married in Vegas. That makes sense. But not really.

I scoff and push him back. "You never even mentioned her name before. Or if you did, I didn't remember. Sorry, I've got a lot going on lately. It's not like you've mentioned anything since that crazy night."

The whole married in Vegas thing still boggles my mind. I still don't understand how Costa would marry a woman he doesn't know. It's just so out of character for him.

Cale tilts his head on an exasperated sigh and rolls his eyes at me.

"I'm pretty sure I've said Sommer's name multiple times. But whatever." He waves a hand, dropping that small point of contention. "She'll be here before the game

Thursday and stay through the weekend. Then she has to get back for her treatment."

The last word tumbles through my head. What treatment is he talking about?

"Huh?" Not the most eloquent response, but hey, the confusion is valid.

Cale swipes his towel over his forehead and shrugs his shoulders.

"Sommer has MS," he explains nonchalantly. At my look of puzzlement, he continues. "Multiple Sclerosis. It's an autoimmune condition that affects the central nervous system. She was just recently diagnosed and is starting some infusion treatment."

"Whoa. That's heavy, bruh. *Wha*—I mean, why—"

Costa swings a leg back over the bench and leans forward, placing his elbows on top of his thighs. Then he runs his hand through his hair, sweeping it away from his face so the scar over his eyebrow is visible. He got it in a game two years ago when I first joined the team. It was a nasty slash of another guy's stick and sent him to the hospital for stitches.

With a lengthy sigh, he drops his chin in one hand and ends up looking like that thinking man statue.

"That night in Vegas, the night I met Sommer, our conversation got deep right away. Like, we instantly connected, you know? And she immediately told me about her diagnosis and how she couldn't afford the monthly treatments." Cale pauses, tightening his jaw through closed eyelids. When he opens his eyes again, they show me exactly what he probably felt that night. "My grandmother... she was poor and my family couldn't do much to help her out besides have her live with us. She died of complications from MS. I know the havoc it wreaks on a body."

I take a seat on the bench across from him, oblivious to all the clanging and noise from the gym around us. I lean forward and mimic Costa's posture.

Cale is one of the nicest guys I've ever met. He's deadly on the ice but has a heart the size of Texas. That heart shines through his friendships, and I know it's what makes him a hell of a great team captain.

It's that compassion that I can only assume led to his marriage.

"Fuck, dude," I acknowledge softly. "Is that the reason you married her? To help her out?"

He shakes his head and turns his gaze toward the gym wall, contemplating something only he can see.

"I know it's difficult to understand, and I appreciate you worrying about me. But yeah, I couldn't just walk away. She's an American, has no family and she's self-employed with crappy, really expensive insurance. I have millions," he says self-deprecatingly, stretching his arms out wide. "I figured it was the least I could do for someone in need."

"I don't know, bruh. That's really kind of you, but did you consider the possibility that she's bullshitting you? She could just be feeding you a line about her health." I click my teeth to show my disapproval.

He shakes his head, rubbing his jawline.

"Nah. She had me sit in on a video call with her doctors, so I know her diagnosis and the treatment are legit. Maybe I'm just a bleeding heart, I don't know." Costa shrugs his shoulders and twists to lie back down across the bench. Turning his head to the side, he lifts his gaze back to mine. "I guess the way I look at it is, if you have the means to help someone else, you gotta do the decent thing. Otherwise, you're just a selfish asshole."

It makes me wonder: If I were put in the same position, would I have the same level of empathy toward a stranger and offer my help?

Or would I be the selfish asshole in that equation?

15

____

Halle

After I finish up the spreadsheet I created with all the new data entered from the most recent game, I check my watch for the fiftieth time in the last six minutes.

12:15 p.m.

Why is it that time ticks by so slowly when you're waiting for something to happen? It's that way when you're counting down the days until your birthday or for Christmas Eve to arrive. Or in this case, for the conversation with your ex about the paternity of your daughter.

Taking a long inhale, I let it go with intention and drop my head back against the chair. Then I begin to touch each finger to my thumbs on each hand, one by one, as a means of calming my nerves.

For five long years I've carried the weight of this secret, one only shared with my dad and Carmen. Not even my brothers know who Lennon's father is, and honestly, they never even bothered to ask. As teenagers, they were too centered on their own lives and playing hockey to wonder about it. That didn't prevent them from being great uncles, though, and they both love Lennon with all their hearts.

My dad, Zack, and Drew all stepped up to be the men she needed in her life. It was an easy topic for me to avoid because she had them to love and dote on her. Until the day came when Lenni expressed an interest in knowing who her daddy was.

It first occurred six months ago when she attended the birthday party of one of her preschool friends. It was held at the little girl's house, and both parents were in attendance and very involved in the event. Lenni came home enamored with the way her friend's dad had entertained them all, even putting on a cute dance performance with his little girl.

When I put Lenni to bed that night, she looked up at me with those soft pewter-gray eyes of hers and asked in her sweet voice, "Mama, will my daddy come to my birthday party, too?"

It shattered my heart into a million irreparable pieces. The response I came up with was not the full truth, and I knew it would only delay the inevitable.

"You don't need one, sweet pea. In fact," I said, brushing her baby soft hair from her face and tucking it behind her ear. "You've got more than just a daddy. You have your Papa and your uncles. You're one lucky girl."

She seemed satisfied with the answer at the time, but I know the question will continue to crop up in the future, possibly leading her to search on her own one day.

Which is why this conversation with Dane is long overdue, regardless of my reluctance to have it.

I'm startled back to the present when my coworker, Anna, who typically works remotely, pops into my cubicle from around the corner.

"Hey, Halle. You've got plans for lunch today?"

She beams at me with hopeful brown eyes. I don't know too much about her yet, since she's been on vacation since I started, but I know we're about the same age and she's engaged to her partner, Mo, short for Molly.

I return Anna's smile with a mopey sad face. "Thank you so much for the offer, Anna. But I have lunch plans to meet up with... an old friend."

This isn't the first time I've been asked out to lunch or a happy hour by my new coworkers. Last week, I went out for a coffee break with Sanita, and was able to grab a drink with a few of our team members one evening while my dad was here. But sadly, going forward, I'm afraid I'll be turning down more invites than I accept. My motherly duties require that I pick up Lenni from her daycare by 6:00 p.m. every night.

My boss, Trevor, has even graciously offered up the babysitting services of his nineteen-year-old daughter, Kelsie, who is earning money to go to New York next summer with a group of students from her school. I told him I'd consider it if needed.

Anna nods with understanding. "No problem. Next time, then. In fact, tomorrow night is Taco Tuesday at the Ale House. Their street tacos are fantastic." She punctuates her sentence with a chef's kiss.

Crap.

I should've known better than to choose a spot where other Vikings employees might frequent. I don't want anyone to see us together and draw the wrong conclusion about me fraternizing with a player. Picking up my phone, I start to type a message to Dane asking that we meet somewhere else, but I've already received a text from him.

> Hockey Boy: I'm here in a booth at the back. See you soon.

"Everything okay?" Anna asks, compassion embedded in her words. "You seem panicked."

I quickly tuck the phone into my jeans pocket and wave with a smile, standing from my desk chair and reaching for my purse hanging on the cubicle wall hook.

"Oh, no, I'm fine, just running late. I'm so sorry I can't go with you today, but I will definitely plan on it next time."

I give Anna's arm a squeeze as I pass her and we go our separate ways. "Have a good lunch."

"You too," she echoes as we walk off in different directions. I hurry into the bathroom to empty my full bladder and double-check my appearance before I head across the street to meet my fate.

THE PUB IS HOPPING as I enter the front door. Although not officially connected to the arena, the Ale House is certainly a hockey-loving pub with strong ties to the team. I give myself a mental slap for not choosing a place a bit more discreet.

Too late now.

I walk past the busy hostess station and weave through the crowd searching for Dane. It's definitely a sports pub with all the team-related photos, gear, and signed jerseys collected over the years on the walls. The entire interior is a hockey fan's dream come true, and I'm sure it's packed on game nights for those who don't have tickets to see the game.

Following the directions Dane texted me, I wind up heading toward a wall in the back corner of the restaurant and soon spot Dane in a booth, his arm draped over the back of the seat, chatting with a long-haired waitress.

Sudden regret washes over me that's so powerful and compelling I nearly turn and walk back out before he sees me.

This is what I have feared all these years. Dane—the Ax Man—Axelrod is a sports hero and celebrity who has fans all over the world, people who think he's larger than life.

If I thought Dane had a big head before he hit the big leagues, I can only assume how much bigger it's become with that level of reverence and adoration he receives from fans and the media. I've heard all about his over-the-top, self-important cellies out on the ice, seen post-game interviews where he doesn't hide his inflated sense of self-worth, and read about the various escapades he has with a revolving door of women.

I'll admit, Dane is an excellent right winger who has become a fan favorite since joining the league. I always knew he would be. And he deserves to be recognized for his skills.

And for his skills off the ice? I don't even think about it.

Okay, maybe that's a little lie.

Perhaps there's a little jealousy permeating my attitude toward Dane. But it shouldn't matter to me. Dane is not mine. I gave up that right to be jealous a long time ago.

Except we're connected still—and will be forever—because of the teeny-tiny fact that Lennon is his daughter.

I am prepared today to shield my daughter from knowing the truth about Dane.

Which means I will clearly explain to him that, while he may have fathered Lennon, we do not want anything from him—not his money or his name. He has no responsibility in this matter whatsoever and should keep it that way.

Honestly, I think it'll be a relief for him. He can walk away without the baggage of a nearly five-year-old little girl to mess up his lifestyle. No harm, no foul. He can go about his free-and-easy life without making any promises he can't keep to us.

I quietly stand behind the waitress, who giggles over something Dane has said. She leans forward over the table in a suggestive manner, and Dane's gaze goes to her cleavage. I clear my throat to announce my presence.

Dane's scandalously flirty smile suddenly morphs into something more cautious and reserved. The woman straightens and twists around, her eyes flickering over me. The corners of her mouth turn up into a half-smile as she looks me over, probably wondering who the hell I am and why I'm here to see Dane.

Don't worry, honey. I'm not in this game.

"Excuse me, I didn't mean to interrupt," I say, offering a polite apology. "Sorry I'm a little late, Dane."

Dane stands from the table and brushes past the waitress—who looks slightly flustered and a tad peeved. Or maybe that's just my assumption based on my past experiences with women who wanted Dane. She moves aside as Dane steps toward me with his arms out wide, and he encloses me in a warm embrace. His spicy scent makes my tummy shimmy with fluttering nerves.

I return the hug by haphazardly wrapping my arms around his waist; he's definitely bigger since the last time I felt him. He's grown into a dedicated athlete who's all hard muscle and broad-shouldered man. That strange thread of awareness returns, and my heart hammers inside my ribs.

Although the hug lasts for only the briefest of moments, I feel his coarse-stubbled jaw rub along my cheek as his face nuzzles into my neck. There's such a familiarity in our embrace, and a small hum of electricity ricochets up my arms. I immediately pull away, caught in a wave of nostalgia and sentiment.

"It's really good to see you, Cherry." He laughs. "I mean, *Halle*. It's been a long time." He gestures to the horseshoe booth, and I scoot in, placing my purse on the empty spot between us.

I inhale deeply and let the breath out, watching him as he tucks his tall body inside the intimate booth.

Now that we're so close, I take a good look at him. Although I've seen him a few times in the last week, I haven't had the opportunity to really appreciate the nuances and changes in his physical appearance.

He's dressed casually in jeans and a plain black T-shirt, the short sleeves showing off the smooth muscles of his biceps. He sweeps a hand through his wavy hair, which is a shade darker and a tad longer than it was in Calgary, allowing him to tuck pieces behind his ears. He used to keep it cut short to his scalp, saying it was easier to manage.

There's a mass of dark stubble covering his strong, angular jaw. Even with the short beard, I can still see that divot in his chin that looks like someone pressed their thumb there upon his birth.

If he had taken a good look at Lennon when he met her, then he must've seen this unique physical attribute they share.

"How are you—" I begin, leaning an elbow on the table to look at him, when he jumps in at the same time with a very different question.

"Is she mine?"

Whoa.

Dane Axelrod does not waste time getting down to business.

He just throws out the easiest to ask, yet most difficult question in the universe for me to answer.

And I'm not sure I'm truly prepared for what will happen when I do.

16

———

Dane

Halle rears back against the seat cushion and blinks, her inky lashes fluttering before she glances to the front door as if looking for an escape.

The suspense is killing me, and her reluctance to tell me is a mystery. Why is it so hard to give me an answer? It's either a yes or no, isn't it?

Does she think I'll be mad? Or be a dick about it and demand a paternity test?

When she finally turns her face to look directly at me, I can see the resolve in her teal-blue eyes. She's always had a confidence about her that made her unflappable. Even when I met her with slushie running down her face, she was embarrassed, sure, but she stood her ground and didn't fall to pieces. It's why I was so attracted to her.

"Yes, she's your daughter. But Dane—"

My breath catches in my lungs, and I cough. "Holy shit."

Her statement hits me harder than a puck to my chest. I thought I was sure of everything, that I'd know how I'd react and respond. I'd be ready to step up and do the right thing. But now the reality of it hits... and I'm speechless.

"Holy shit," I mumble again, still trying to find my words and unable to fully comprehend this entire situation. "I'm a dad?"

"Dane, listen to me." Halle stretches her arm across the table, her hand balled in a fist.

I look down at it and wonder if she wants me to hold it. But instead, she opens her fingers and deposits a small white box in front of me. The air gets trapped in my lungs, and I stare at it and then back at her. Her eyes search mine. "I completely understand if you want to confirm Lennon's paternity before discussing this any further."

I pick up the box and read the label. *DNA Paternity At-Home Test Kit.* Something inside me ignites an irrational urge to throw the box out the window.

Instead, I shove it back in Halle's direction. Her eyes flash questioningly, with a hint of confusion.

"I don't need this to know."

"Dane," she says, shaking her head. "Be reasonable. It's for your own peace of mind and leaves no room for doubt."

I knead an eyebrow with my fingertips, tipping my

head to one side and pinning her with my gaze. "I trust you, Halle. I know you wouldn't lie or bullshit me about this."

Halle sighs, her shoulders deflating like a balloon letting out its air.

But fuck me. I want to be honest with my feelings here. And while I know she's not fucking lying to me, she has omitted the truth for five years. How do I respond to that?

"But why the hell didn't you ever tell me you got pregnant?" My words sound more accusatory than I mean them to. Misty the waitress chooses this moment to return with the water and her expression clearly tells me she just heard what I said. And from the looks from the table across from us, I may not have used my inside voice with that announcement.

Fuck. TMZ is going to be running this on their six o'clock episode tonight.

I cast a glance at Misty and raise my eyebrows in a silent request for her to remain discreet. She takes the cue and flees the table, looking over her shoulder at us once more before leaving me alone with Halle, whose eyes swim with unshed tears.

I inch closer to her in the U-shaped booth, moving her purse out of the way, and throw my arm behind the upholstered seat. I squeeze my hand into a tight fist, digging my nails into my palm to fend off the urge to stroke her silky hair.

"Please, Halle." I reach for her hand currently toying

with a napkin on the table. "Why did you keep this from me? I don't understand."

She inhales a deep breath and blows it out, wiping away a tear that had escaped down her cheek.

"I'm sorry, Dane," she says, her voice quavering a bit from emotion. She clears her throat and straightens her posture against the booth. "The thing is, I honestly never wanted you to find out about Lenni."

I'm stunned, literally stunned by her admission. I extract my arm from behind her and clasp my hands together on the table, then slide them forward. Rounding my back, I drop my head in disbelief.

I slowly turn to give her a side glance, searching for something in her expression that will explain her logic for keeping this secret from me.

Halle leans forward and reaches out to curl her palms over my fists. Her touch—so gentle and hesitant—confuses me. It makes me want to curl into her and make her mine again. But on the other hand, it's patronizing and judging.

"Please understand my position," she says imploringly, lips quivering. But I yank my hands away and jerk back upright, staring off in front of me so I can avoid her gaze.

"Jesus Christ, Halle." The words come out like an arrow. "How did you think so little of me? Did I ever do anything to make you believe I wouldn't have been there for you?"

Halle shakes her head, and strands of hair fall

around her face. She tucks some behind her ears and moves toward me until there's only a few inches between us. Her honey-and-lavender scent surrounds me, like an intoxicating force field that has me frozen in time.

"No, that's not what I believed at all. But life was complicated after I found out I was pregnant with Lenni. I was dealing with big emotions and wild mood swings." Her brows furrow and the corners of her mouth dip down into a frown. She slides her hands under the table, and I can see her absently picking her nails. "I not only lost my scholarship but didn't have a way to return to school. I was scared out of my mind about how my dad would react to my pregnancy and what he'd say. And then, after dealing with those stresses, when I was finally at a place where I could tell you... by then, you'd been drafted."

I'll admit, it sounds like she'd had a lot on her plate to go through alone. It only hurts more that she didn't choose to reach out right away. I would've been by her side.

Wouldn't I?

I shift to face her and adjust my legs so my knees don't bump into hers. I'm not sure if either one of us could handle any physical connection right now.

"You had plenty of time to let me know." I count out the months on my fingers. "April. May. June."

She nods her head. "Yeah, I suppose I did. Trust me, I vacillated at least fifteen times a day. Pregnancy hormones are no joke. I drove my family nuts." Halle laughs at her own inside joke.

Fuck it. I need to touch her.

I reach under the table and capture her hand in mine, holding it on the seat between us. Her skin is so soft, and a little cold. Such a contrast from my hot, callused hands. I stare down at her short, pink-painted nails and wonder how much she's been through without me to support her.

"I promised you, Cherry. Remember? I thought that meant something."

Halle wiggles her fingers loose from my grip but then intertwines her slim fingers through mine.

"I know, Dane. But it was the promise of an eighteen-year-old on the cusp of a very big life. I did this for you as much as I did it for Lennon." She looks at me with frank earnestness. "Be real. You would have never been around to see her. You played for Chicago at the time, and we were in Calgary. How would that have even worked?"

I make a scoffing noise of protest, my ego taking the hit even though I know she's probably right.

Professional hockey is hard when you're on the road at least nine months a year, in and out of cities across North America and sometimes playing games in other countries. I've seen how hard it is for the guys with families when they're on the road. Even when they're home, they don't have much time to spend quality time with their families or significant others.

"Still," I argue, lifting my chin in indignation. "At the

very least, you could've told me. I could've supported you financially at least."

Halle fidgets in the booth seat, her gaze lifting to mine. In it, I see my pain reflecting back on me.

"I texted you that June," she states softly. My eyes narrow. "Your draft day. But you never responded. Maybe I didn't expect you to, but I gave up. I told myself that you'd moved on and I wouldn't ever try contacting you again."

"What text?" I prod. That day had been a whirlwind.

I was in LA with my parents and my agent, sitting through the first round, sweating through my new suit and biting my nails as I waited for my name to be called. My agent was honest and told me he hadn't expected me to be selected that early on. I was an excellent right winger with solid stats from juniors, but there was tough competition that year, and we both knew that being drafted in the first round was a pipe dream.

If I thought waiting through the first round was tough, the first half of the second round was utter torture. But then the Chicago Buoys had their next pick, and the owner read off my name. I can't even begin to describe the elation inside me when my name was read and my lifelong dream of becoming a pro hockey player was fulfilled.

Everything was chaos from that moment on. I was ushered up to a podium at the front of a large arena filled with thousands of players, parents, members of the press, and sports fans. My hands had become clammy, and I rubbed them down my suit pants before meeting the owner and GM of the Buoys, who shook my hand and gave me pats on the back. I was given a jersey and a turquoise Buoys hat—which, strangely enough, had brought Halle to mind. Then I was ushered off to a formal meeting where I signed my exclusive intent to play for the team.

All that was followed by ceremonies, media interviews, photoshoots, and parties in a hotel suite with members of the team and staff. It was a blur of people.

The truth is, if Halle had sent me a text that day or even in the days that followed, I likely did miss it amongst the hundreds I received.

Sadly, one missed text led to missing out on a whole lot of Lennon's life.

Halle regards me thoughtfully, as if trying to figure something out. I keep my expression neutral, even though I'm boiling on the inside. There are so many questions demanding to be answered, but we don't have time to resolve them all today. I'm not sure where we will even go from here.

"I'm not going to lie, Dane. It broke my heart."

"It wasn't intentional, I swear." I raise my hands in defense and pin her with an apologetic gaze. She nods once.

"Okay, fine," she acquiesces, flitting one hand in the air. "But I remained cautiously hopeful I'd hear back from you at some point. And when that response never came, it felt like defeat. Like I never mattered to you. So I blocked your number."

Halle dips her head and makes a face, tightening her mouth contritely.

"Seriously? You must have known how I felt about you," I say, hoping to justify my position. "If you remember, you were the one who broke things off with me. I didn't want to but went along with it for your sake. Had we still been together, I would've known and none of this would've ever happened."

The minute the censorious words leave my mouth, and I see the hurt expression and pain in her eyes, I know it was a dick thing to say. I inhale deeply and rub a hand over the stubble on my cheeks.

Fuck, I'm botching this up so bad.

She reaches for her purse and starts to get up from the booth, but I grasp her wrist to keep her from leaving. Halle gives me a look, and I drop my hand.

"Halle, please. Don't go. I'm sorry. That came out wrong."

This can't be the end of this conversation. I don't want her to go. We need to figure this out and resolve things if we are going to move forward. Because if I've learned anything from this news, it's that I want to be part of both her and Lennon's lives.

"Halle, I know none of this is your fault, and I didn't mean to make it sound otherwise. It was just bad timing and circumstances that messed everything up. I'm sorry I made you feel like I didn't care about you. I promise you, I would've been there for you."

Halle's gaze drifts back to mine and she gives me a meaningful look, her teal eyes sparkling with diamond tears as a watery smile appears on her face.

"I know. You may have been a hockey boy with a big ego, but you were never an asshole."

I laugh at the nickname she gave me when we first met and raise a brow.

Misty returns to the table to take down our orders, giving us a few moments to reflect and step away from the heaviness of our conversation.

This entire discussion is surreal, and I can't quite wrap my head around the fact that I am someone's *father*. Lennon is my daughter. I don't need a paternity test to know the truth, although I know what my dad and agent will tell me.

Take the fucking test.

And then a thought occurs to me.

Halle said earlier that she never wanted me involved in Lennon's life before this. But what about now? Is she willing to let me in now?

I didn't even know Lenni even existed before. But now that I do, I'm here and she's here. I'm ready to take on the responsibility of being her dad.

I place my elbows on the table and cup my chin in my hands, quirking one eyebrow skyward.

"Okay, so what's next? When do we tell Lennon I'm her dad?"

17

Halle

My surprise over Dane's eager question is only surpassed by my shock at the appearance of Anna at our table. I feel trapped in a situation that could blow up unnecessarily and turn into a huge tornado of rumor.

Exactly what I'd hoped to avoid.

"Hey, Halle," Anna says in greeting, barely able to contain the surprised grin on her face. Her eyes gleam with curiosity as her gaze flicks between me and Dane. Extending a hand to Dane, she wraps the most artistically done nails I've ever seen around his knuckles when he offers his in return.

I'm momentarily dazzled with the daydream of what it would be like to have an hour to myself to spend at a nail salon. Or anywhere I can have a bit of quiet time for myself.

I brush the thought away and watch the two of them.

"Nice to officially meet you, Ax. I'm Anna Morris. I'm an analyst with Halle down in the Cave."

The Cave, I learned last week, is the name the Ops team calls our area of the office because it's a whole floor below the ice. It's where all the loot—aka the team data—is stored, which is a goldmine of information the team uses to get a leg up on their opponents. And since the Vikings were notorious for looting and pillaging for riches, the Cave was a natural nickname.

Dane stands up as best he can in the cramped booth and returns the greeting with a bright smile, clearly not knocked off-balance like I am. Of course, he's not the one who will be answering all the questions from coworkers when I return to the office.

"Oh, right. Yeah, I've seen your last name before on our reporting notes. Good to meet you."

A trickle of nervous sweat beads in the middle of my back. How am I going to explain this to Anna? Will she go back and start rumors about me and Dane? She doesn't seem like someone who would do that, but one never knows.

Anna adjusts the strap of her purse and looks over her shoulder.

"I was just about to get back when I noticed you both back here. So..." She blinks and cocks her head. "Dane's the old friend you mentioned, eh?"

Anxiety floods my veins and my heart gallops faster

than you can say Sidney Crosby. Being seen out like this could easily be misconstrued like Dane and I are together. I snap my gaze to Dane, my eyes sending a silent plea to stay quiet about how we know each other as he returns to his spot next to me.

Without even an ounce of hesitation, Dane launches into an animated story of how we met.

"Halle and I know each other from Calgary. We're just catching up, aren't we, Hal?" He turns that oh-so-charming smile on me, the divot-dimple doubling in size. Then he throws his arms around me in a huge bear hug and tips me back and forth in an outrageous display of fondness.

I can't help myself. When he lets me go, I kick him under the table and he laughs out loud.

Anna eyes him quizzically, as if trying to decide whether to believe him.

"Aww, I bet it's been fun to catch up. I bet a lot has changed since then."

I smile innocently. "You have no idea."

Dane laughs loudly and Anna smiles at us both, still trying to put two and two together by the look in her eyes, just as Misty appears behind Anna with our order.

"That's our food." I motion with my chin to the tray of food being placed on the table. "I'll see you back in the Cave in twenty, Anna."

She turns away for a second, looking back at the door where her friend waits to leave. "Sounds good. I'll see you in a bit. And nice to meet you, Ax." She wiggles goodbye with her fingers. "Have a great lunch, you two."

Her words come out in a conspiratorial coo. Not knowing Anna very well, I don't know how to interpret it. But so far, she's been very friendly and helpful, so I hope she doesn't read anything into witnessing Dane and me together.

Without sparing her another look, Dane immediately digs into the food placed in front of him, gobbling down the club sandwich and poutine fries he ordered. I gape at him devouring his lunch.

"How do you do that without choking to death?" I shake my head in amusement, amazed at how he can wolf down food without chewing a single bite.

He shrugs. "It's a learned skill, Cherry."

And then he winks.

"Some things never change," I muse, over both his eating habits and that damn wink.

My stomach flutters wildly, and I stab a piece of my crab salad and shove it into my mouth. Regardless of the reason we're here together, there's no getting by how ridiculously attractive and charismatic Dane is.

This entire scene reminds me of the morning we first had breakfast together in Calgary and how easily he won me over. All through high school, I'd been staunchly opposed to dating anyone who played sports, especially hockey.

My God, hockey players can be an arrogant lot. What with my brothers and their friends, I've been around enough of them to pick up the types of conversations they have. It's not unusual for them to talk about their sexual prowess and exploits, but there was no way I ever wanted the intimacies of my sex life or body discussed by a team of horny dudes.

It was the night of Carmen's holiday party when I made the bold decision to lose my virginity with Dane. While I was desperate to lose my V-card before college, I wouldn't have slept with Dane if I hadn't known in my heart that he was a good guy and would protect my secrets.

He had dispelled the myth of the cocky, self-centered, hockey boy.

Which made my decision to break it off before college even more difficult. But I did it out of self-preservation. I wanted my heart to survive intact.

The irony is that by the time my heart started to mend and the dreams I had about Dane had waned, the little blue plus sign made its appearance on a pregnancy stick.

I'm only halfway through my salad when Dane wipes his mouth with his napkin and starts back where we left off before our lunch was served.

"Can I ask you a question?" His voice is solemn, and his gray eyes have softened. I've always loved the way his eyes could change in their coloring, exactly the way Lenni's do.

I nod, placing my fork down on my plate. "Of course."

He rubs a hand over the scruff of his cheek and expels a breath. "Why did you decide to keep the baby?"

My forehead furrows with confusion.

"You mean, why didn't I end the pregnancy or give her up for adoption?"

Dane shoves his hands in his hair and places his elbow on the table. "I don't want it to sound judgmental or like I'm suggesting you should have. That's not what I mean..." He lifts his head again and stares at me with sincerity in his eyes. "I just remember how excited you were about playing volleyball in college and getting your degree. A baby must have complicated that."

I snort. "Ya think?"

He makes a face. "Yeah. I can't imagine what it must've been like for you. If I'd been in your shoes and had to give up hockey? *Fuck.*"

Pursing my lips together, I avoid his eyes while considering my response carefully. I look off into the bustling restaurant, recalling when I worked as a hostess while pregnant.

"My life would be a lot different, that's for sure. But not better. I guess the universe took matters into her own hands and removed that decision from me because by the time I found out, I was too far along." I turn and lock my eyes with his. "And honestly? Lenni is the best thing that has ever happened to me. I love being her mom."

The life she's brought me flashes before my eyes. The moment I first saw her small form appear on the ultrasound, her tiny bean-like body curled up like a shrimp.

The day I felt the first kick in my belly. Holding her in the delivery room after a twelve-hour labor. Watching her take her first steps as she toddled from me to my dad on our living room floor.

Hearing the sound of her giggles as she ran down the hallway at full speed. The sweet tone in her voice when she says, "Mama."

My heart tripled in size the day she came into my life.

"I wouldn't change it for the world," I say with finality. "It's true what they say. Sometimes the hardest parts of your life are what prepare you for the greatest."

Dane smiles and leans toward me. "Let me be part of it, Hal. Please."

God, how do I say no to such a heartfelt request?

"Let me think about it. Just give me some time, okay?"

He looks dejected but then his mouth curves up into a smile that melts my insides. After he pays the check, he places a hand at the small of my back as we head outside into the gray and misty afternoon.

When was the last time a man touched me like that?

I expect him to walk with me across the street toward the arena, but he stops at the corner and turns to me instead.

The next thing I know, I'm enveloped in his warm embrace. I want to bury my nose in his chest and never come up for air. He smells like man and pine tree and something spicy yet sweet. Like brown sugar and bourbon. It's an intoxicating combination, and I can't help but return the hug.

With his mouth close to my ear, he whispers so softly that the words are nearly drowned out by the traffic and street noise.

"I'll be here for you and Lenni when you're ready." He kisses the top of my head and the world tilts underneath my feet. "I promise you."

18

———

D ane

"It's your call, dickhead."

I snap my gaze up from the five cards I have fanned in my hand and look through the haze of stogie smoke for the source of the interruption. It was Rossco, who sits to my right at the poker table and who is guffawing over my lack of attention.

"Jesus Christ, Ax. I don't know where your head is tonight—probably up your ass—but keep it up, bruh, and I'm going home a rich man."

The guys all laugh and snicker at his typical nonsensical comment. I scoff with a severe roll of my eyes.

"You already are a rich fucker, Rossy." I retort, flipping him off and then mean-mugging the four other guys at the table. "So are all of you, motherfuckers." Because every one of us at this game table are multimillion-dollar players. Well, except Case and Shaw, the rookies. They're both still at league minimum, having been just called up from the minors.

Tonight's our monthly poker game at Case Lyons's and Shaw Bennings's shared condo.

It's become something of a rite of passage for each season's rookies to host the regular parties at their place. It's our way of getting them to step up and be part of the team off the ice. It's also fun to have them wait on us hand and foot. Although, Costa makes all of us chip in to cover the tab for the food and drinks so it's not on the rookies' dime.

But tonight is not my night for much of anything. I've already lost three hands in a row, and my chips are dwindling fast.

With a sigh of annoyed defeat, I lay my cards face down on the poker table with a curse. "Fuck, I'm out. I fold."

Through hoots and hollers, and even a "Fuck yeah" from Brewer, I slink back in my chair and run a hand through my mussed-up hair. I'm not even sure I combed it after we finished our workouts earlier.

For being the most obtuse on the team, Rossco's not wrong about me. I do have my head in the clouds. That's not to say I haven't been killing it on the ice, even scoring goals in each of our three last games, but outside of that, all I can do is wait impatiently for Halle's answer.

I've been called a lot of things in my life but patient is not one of them. It's been over two weeks now since our lunch, and it's been complete radio silence. I'm not sure how much longer I can hack it without hearing from her.

The night after we had lunch, I took the paternity test and sent it directly to the lab. Within a week it was confirmed that Lenni is indeed my daughter. Without a shred of doubt.

Honestly, I knew it subconsciously the first time I met Lennon and then once Halle confirmed it, even before I'd even received the results. And I didn't waste time letting Halle know either.

> Me: I just got the results back. 99.9% positive.

> Me: So, have you given it more thought? Can we talk?

It took her a good hour to finally respond to me that night, and all I got back from her was a valid excuse to delay.

> Cherry: Not now. Lenni has been running a temp and feeling sick.

Having never been around a sick kid, I wasn't sure what that meant exactly, but I wanted her to know I was available if she needed me.

> Me: Call me if I can help out. Hope she gets better soon.

> Cherry: Thanks.

That was the last I heard from her, and that was five days ago. Shouldn't a kid be better by now? I googled it and then started to worry profusely when I saw the list of all the terrible things that can make a child sick.

Part of me wants to call Halle and demand she tell me what was going on with our daughter. I'm ready to fucking go. I want to be there for both Halle and Lennon.

But I also want to respect Halle's boundaries. She's been a parent for over four years while I've known for less than a week that I've fathered a child. I have zero experience to draw on, so I've kept a tight rein on my demands and expectations. I told her I would wait for her and I will, even though it's making me a grump to be around tonight.

And that honor usually goes to Wolf.

I'm so lost in my thoughts that I don't hear my phone ring from my jeans pocket. Wolf nudges me in my side.

"Bruh, isn't that your phone?"

I snap my head at him, and he lifts his eyebrows.

"Uh, yeah. Thanks." I pull out the phone and stare down at the name that lights up on the display.

Cherry

Holy shit. Is this happening now?

I stand up with so much force that I knock the chair off its legs and then step back from the table.

"I gotta take this." I waggle my phone in the air, as if my teammates don't understand what a person does with a ringing phone. Then I lift my chin toward Lyons, who is on the couch with a game controller in his hands and playing some war game with Canners, who surprised us all by showing up tonight.

"Yo, Canners. You want to take my spot next round? I'm out."

Cannfield flicks his gaze away from the giant-screen TV and gives me a look, gesturing with his chin toward the screen. "Fuck off. I'm beating the rookie right now."

I shrug my shoulder and head toward the sliding glass door that leads to the rookies' deck. Which is eight floors up from the ground. I'm not big on heights, so I stay close to the wall as I step outside and answer the call.

"Hello? Halle?"

The line is silent for a moment and then I hear a sickly moan.

"Dane..." she croaks out, thick and hoarse, but not in any sensual way. More like she's rasping for air. I can hear her lungs rattle.

I'm immediately on high alert. Her voice is usually chipper and bubbly, often with a bit of sarcasm. Had it not been her contact's name on my display, I wouldn't have recognized her. She does not sound good at all.

"Cherry? What's going on?" I say, panic and dread icing through my limbs.

I hear something on the other end of the line that sounds vaguely like Lenni singing a song in the background.

"I... really... sick," she groans out, the words stumbling out of her like they cost her dearly to say each one. "Need sleep. Need you."

Hearing those words is enough to fill me with superhuman strength. I will take a flying leap off this eighth-floor balcony just to be there because she asked. I will be there to do whatever she needs from me.

"Send me your address, I'll be right there."

THE GUYS barely bat an eye when I tell them I have to leave unexpectedly. Rossco provides his own commentary on my departure, stating I was probably heading out to meet up with two hot chicks who would console me over my horrible loss tonight.

Well, he got part of that right.

I plug in the address Halle sent me and consider what I might find when I get to her house.

She sounded terrible and out of it, like maybe she was even delirious from fever.

I don't know anything about how to take care of someone else when they're sick. The only experience I've ever had was when one of my former juniors teammates, Beau Withers, got wasted on Rumple Minze shots and puked all over the shared bathroom of our hotel. I had to clean that shit up, and to this day, if I get one whiff of that noxious mint flavor, I end up gagging.

My map app tells me I'm less than two blocks away from her neighborhood, and as I near the street I'm slated to turn onto, I notice a small convenience store on the corner.

I flip on my signal and turn into the parking lot. I park haphazardly in front of the store and run in to search for some kind of cold and flu remedies, maybe a carton of orange juice and some premade soup.

While I wait for the seemingly bored-out-of-his-mind checkout clerk to scan through my haul, I see some kids' toys on the display rack over the conveyor belt and add one to my purchases.

Heading back to the car, I pull out of the lot and turn down a quiet residential street with small, similar-looking ramblers and bungalows lining both sides of the tree-lined road. I peer at each house number until I find hers.

Once I reach her small, white, one-story home, I turn into a short, paved driveway. A detached garage with the door shut tight sits further back behind the house, and a chain-link fence wraps around the backyard. Although it's dark, I see a tricycle and some toys strewn across the yard and smile to myself.

I'm glad Lenni has a safe place to play. I park my car in the driveway next to the small bungalow and turn off the engine. Opening the car door, I unload the bag of groceries to the sounds of neighborhood dogs barking at my appearance.

Walking toward the front door, I'm hit with a niggle of worry in my stomach.

I'm not sure what Halle expects from me tonight, but going in cold has me a bit worried if I can handle it.

I push the anxiety away and climb the three cement

block steps that lead to her front door, giving myself a pep talk. I play against some of the toughest two-hundred-pound men in the league, and I've managed to deke, outskate, and outscore them with ease.

This will be a piece of cake.

Shifting the bag into the crook of my left arm, I ring the security doorbell and wait.

Tiny footsteps padding to the door can be heard from inside, and I inhale a breath, expelling it slowly as the door creaks open and I come face-to-face with my daughter.

Lennon's face is covered in what looks like an explosion of chocolate, like she took a bath in a tub of Hershey syrup.

She looks up at me with those wide eyes the same color and shape of mine, blinking rapidly as if she's trying to remember how she knows me.

"Hey, Lennon."

"My mama's sick," she explains by way of greeting, her mouth turning down into a slight frown.

I kneel on one leg so I'm down at her level and place the bag of groceries next to my foot.

"I know. I'm sorry to hear that. I'm Ax, remember me?"

She tips her head to the side and considers this information. Then she gives a swift nod and swings the door open, taking off into the room and leaving me out on the front step. I pick up the bag and stand, peering into the house after her.

"Halle?" I call out quietly, scanning the front room and the kitchen next to it to see if she's around. But the only things I see are a pile of throw blankets on the couch and a mess of toys on the floor in every direction. It looks like a tornado upended the toy box and threw everything across the room.

"Lennon, where's your mommy?" I ask as I place the grocery bag on the kitchen table. I crane my neck down a small hallway that looks like it leads to the bedrooms and try to listen for any noise coming from the back of the house.

Lenni swivels around and points to the long couch that faces a TV and fireplace lining the wall. And sure enough, it's then that I notice a tuft of messy auburn hair sticking out from underneath. To further confirm it's her, the blankets shift when her body shakes with a coughing fit.

"Come play a game with me, Ax," Lenni demands, seemingly unfazed by her mother's state of distress as she grabs my hand to lead me into the living room.

And that's all it takes. Apparently, four-year-olds need no further proof or formal identification when looking for a friend to play with.

Looks like my first task in dad mode will be to discuss the topic of stranger danger.

19

———

Dane

Lenni drops my hand and scurries in mismatched socks across hardwood floors to plop down in front of a pink play castle on the floor.

She glances back at me with a look of censure because I'm still paused at the edge of the couch, wondering if I should check on Halle.

"I'm the pwincess," she informs me without room for disagreement, and holds up a small yellow-haired plastic doll wearing a blue dress and a crown. "You be Olaf."

She giggles at her own private joke that I'm clearly not in on. I look off into the direction of the kitchen, which is also in a state of disarray. If I had to guess— knowing Halle's penchant for organization—this isn't how it usually looks. That means things have been bad for days. There are open cereal boxes, a tub of animal crackers, empty juice boxes, and an array of bowls and utensils laying out across the table and countertops.

"Okay, Lenni," I say, offering a placating smile. "I'll come play with you in a little bit. But first I need to put these groceries away and then take care of your mommy. Do you want to help me with that?"

"No, I'm good."

I can't help but chuckle at her blunt and unfiltered response. But she seems appeased for the moment, so I kneel next to the couch and place a gentle hand on top of the blanket where I think Halle's shoulder should be. The blankets rustle and Halle moans.

"Halle? It's me. I'm here."

Another muffled moan emits from under the blankets, and I pull the covers back to expose a small portion of her face. Her eyes are closed, and her eyelids appear glued shut, eyelashes matted and crusty from sleep. Her normally cherry red lips are dry and cracked. Dark circles color underneath her eyes, and her hairline is dotted with sweat.

I do what my mom always did when I was sick and place the back of my hand against her forehead.

She's fucking burning up.

"Halle, I'm going to get you something to drink and then put you to bed, okay?"

Another whimper and I rush off into the kitchen, rooting around in the cupboards for two clean glasses. Finding them, I fill one with cold water from the tap and the other with a small amount of the OJ I brought.

When I return to the living room, I find Lenni singing along with a song that's playing on a tablet propped up on a sofa table. Thank God for electronics. The best babysitters in the world.

I set the glasses on the table and look down at Halle's sleepy form.

"Can you sit up for me, Hal?"

"Mm-hmm."

I wait for a second, but she makes no attempt to move. Taking matters into my own hands, I gently remove the blankets off her upper torso and lean down to wedge my hands behind her back. She makes a noise of protest as I try to get her to sit up.

Now that I have a good look at her, I realize just how sick and out of it she is. I'm pretty sure it's the fever that's gotten her so out of sorts, and while I'm not some miracle worker, at least I can make sure she gets some much-needed rest and fluids while I'm here.

Keeping a steadying hand on her shoulder to keep her upright and stable, I reach behind me for the glass of water and bring it to her parched lips. Her eyes are still closed and puffy, her nose a red, snotty mess.

"Can you take a sip of the water for me?"

She makes no attempt to lift her hands to the glass, so I hold it in place and tip it forward as she takes two, maybe three, tiny sips and then sputters in a coughing fit.

Damn, this isn't going to be as easy as I thought.

I look around and, finding a box of tissues on the side

table, grab a few sheets. I wipe away the water from her mouth just as her head flops back against the couch cushion like it weighs a hundred pounds.

"That's good, baby. We'll try again in a little while. Let's get you to bed."

Out of the corner of my eye, I can see that Lenni has stopped with her make-believe play for the moment and watches me with interest.

"My mama's not a baby," she says adamantly.

It takes me a second to understand what she means as I work to wrench the twisted covers away from Halle's legs.

I give her a short reply. "Oh, right. Sorry."

Slipping one arm behind her back and the other under her knees, I scoop Halle up and lift her from the couch. Her body is deadweight in my arms.

"Hey, Lenni? Can you show me where your mommy's room is?" I ask, starting down the hallway toward where the bedrooms must be.

I'm sure I can figure it out on my own, but this way, Lenni can be involved.

Lenni jumps up from her spot and rushes ahead of me, giving me a play-by-play lay of the land as we make our way down the hall.

"This is my bedroom. It has a pwincess bed." She points at the small room to the right that's painted a bright bubblegum pink. And sure enough, there is indeed a princess bed, fully accessorized with one of those sheer canopies covering the head of the bed frame. It even has twinkle lights. Exactly how I'd picture a little girl's room to be decorated.

A thought slams straight through my heart. Halle is a wonderful mom to Lenni.

It sparks a seed of doubt inside me. Would I have ever thought of doing something like this for Lenni? What if I'm not equipped to handle being a girl dad? I don't know anything at all about little kids unless they play hockey. Maybe someday soon I can teach her to play, too.

I shake those thoughts away for now as we move past her room and the bathroom, then into the bedroom at the end of the hallway.

Other than a few baby photos of Lenni, a picture of Halle and Lenni together, and a family picture with Lenni wearing a red coat being held by one of her uncles as they pose in front of a giant outdoor Christmas tree, the room is sparsely decorated. The Christmas scene looks vaguely familiar, however. I think I went to that exact location once when I lived with my billet family. It's the annual tree-lighting ceremony at the local community township center.

Other than that, the room has a closet that sports a broken slatted door hanging off its hinges and unopened moving boxes stacked inside.

As I skirt around some scattered clothes on the floor, Halle sniffles and mutters something into my chest that sounds like "I've missed you."

It could be wishful thinking on my part that she still has feelings for me too. Or it could be just some fever-dream nonsense said in a fog of illness and a fever, but I can't help but preen under the weight of the statement.

"I've missed you, too, Cherry," I whisper back, kissing the top of her head.

I gently lay her down and grab the edge of the blanket at her feet, dragging it up her legs and covering her torso. As I try to tuck her arms inside, Halle's hands spring up and loop around my head, catching me off guard. With surprising strength for a woman half my size and under the effects of a virus, she tugs me down into a tight hug.

"Dane... the only one." The words are spoken so softly, and without context, that I barely understand them.

The only one what?

Then her hands slip from my neck, and, exhausted from the energy it took to hold them there, she closes her eyes, rolling on her side and falling back to sleep almost instantly.

I brush the hair from her face and place another kiss on the top of her forehead before I leave the room. A quick check on Lenni, who is still playing with her doll and castle, and I return to the bedroom a few moments later, glasses of juice and water in hand, and place them next to Halle on her bedside table.

When I set them down, I notice a painted jewelry box with its lid partially propped open. Only a few items are inside. A set of pearls that maybe belonged to her mom. A pair of gold hoop earrings. And a plastic hockey puck key ring.

I squint and pick it up, examining it in my hand.

Nah, it couldn't be.

Flipping it around my finger, I study it further as memories resurface of a date when we played games at an arcade. Having won enough game tickets for a prize, this was the one she picked out, so I got it for her.

Why would she have kept this cheap trinket all these years?

Unless... it holds meaning.

A memento of some kind to remember me? I rub a palm over my stubbled jaw and consider the words she just spoke—even if she hadn't been quite lucid—and try to piece together what it all could mean.

The only one... What, though?

It would make sense, I suppose, that she could've meant I'm the only one she could call tonight. I'm likely the only person she knows in Vancouver who could help her out in a pinch, so logically, that calculates.

But my gut needs a deeper meaning hidden in the words, one that connects our past with the present.

What if she meant I'm the only one she would trust to take care of her and Lenni?

I consider that as a plausible explanation, mulling it over in my head as I replace the keepsake back into the box where I found it.

Something niggles inside me, though, and I theorize one more explanation.

What if she meant that I'm the only one she's ever loved?

I don't have time to examine that theory, though, because a tiny hand reaches for my wrist and tugs me out the doorway.

"Come on, Ax. Time to play wiff me."

20

————

Halle

I wake slowly and, with Herculean effort, pry my eyelids open. But as soon as I do, the room swims in a gauzy haze, like I'm looking through murky waters. My lids fall closed again.

The next time I wake up, it's because, from somewhere beyond my conscious state and bedroom, I hear laughter.

It's the sound of my daughter's sweet giggle followed by a deep, resonating chuckle.

I bolt upright in bed, the sweat of panic beading in the hollow of my throat. The move is clearly the wrong one because a sharp pain hits me squarely between my brows, nearly knocking me back over. My stomach rolls with nausea. I manage to prop a hand behind me and steady my head with the other.

Taking deep breaths, I slowly exhale and take stock of my current state.

Blankets are thrown around the bed, and my sheets and pajamas are saturated and sticky from sweat. I give an experimental sniff at my underarm and practically recoil from the stale, nasty stench.

Regardless of my current state of dress and odor, my immediate priority is checking on the safety and well-being of Lenni.

I untangle my legs from the blankets, using energy I don't have to throw the covers back and swing my legs over to the side of the bed, my bare feet touching the floor. Once again, my body betrays me, and my head lolls forward in a wave of dizziness. I groan and swallow down the bile that threatens to escape my throat.

The next minute—or it could be ten because right now time is an unknown quantity—a large, masculine body appears beside me, hands positioned on my shoulders to hold me upright. My head swirls in dizziness, the edges of my vision bursting with white light.

"Hang on there, Cherry. Let me help you."

With strength I didn't know I possessed, I tilt my head and peer into Dane's earnest gray eyes.

I lick my dry lips and try to speak through a parched mouth.

"Lenni?" I croak out, the words like fire from my burning throat.

Those gray eyes crinkle and his mouth curves at the corners to offer me a smile.

"She's doing great. I have her coloring at the table right now, but she's dying to get out on her bicycle."

My body sags in relief. And then I'm hit with another panicked thought, and my heart bottoms out in my stomach.

I gasp. "What day is it? How long have you been here? And when...?"

Before he can answer, Lenni runs into my room, bringing with her a barrage of happy, high-pitched chatter.

"Mama! You're awake, Mama!" She tries to reach up on her tiptoes to hug me, but I shift my weight to pull away, and Dane puts out a hand to stop her.

"Hold up there, Lulu Lennon," he says with such familiarity that I want to cry. "Your mommy is still really sick."

Technically, I got this bug from her. With her starting the new daycare a few weeks back, she brought all the ick germs home with her. I'm just thankful my sweet girl didn't get as sick as I am with this virus. There is nothing worse than when you have a child sick in your arms and there is nothing you can do but wait it out.

Disappointment washes over her face, her smile dampening until Dane lifts her up in his arms, then she grins wildly.

My ovaries dance and flip at the sight of him doting on my daughter. *Our* daughter.

For five years, I managed to avoid this very image in my head because I never wanted—or expected—it to happen. To me, it would be the worst if he swooped in, stole her heart, and then left her devastated when he got bored and left us.

I've seen it too many times to friends who were children of divorce. The mothers were left to pick up the pieces while the dads just left their families behind.

Nothing in this world can be as damaging to a child's psyche than loving their father and then losing that relationship when he moves away and on with his life.

And shit. It might already be too late because I can see how Lenni looks adoringly at Dane.

My heart clenches in fear, and I want to protect her own heart from that pain.

On the positive, at least she doesn't know Dane is her father. And I need it to stay that way. For the present time, Dane can just be her good friend, Ax.

"It's okay, Mama. I'm not sick. Ax gave me my witamins and milk so I can be strong." Lenni flexes her little bicep to prove she's immune. "And Mama, he played Olaf with me. And we watched Moana. And we played hockey. And he made me pancakes wiff lots of surr-up. But not bananas. I told him I don't like those."

She shakes her head and wrinkles her nose in an icky face of disgust. Lenni has always been a good eater, trying almost anything I put in front of her. She's a huge fan of broccoli, tomatoes, peas, even bell peppers, eating them like candy. But it's the smell and texture of bananas she's never been able to get over.

I want to laugh but my chest hurts too much, and I fear I'll start in on another coughing fit if I do.

I work my lips into what I think is a cracked-lip smile instead. "That's good, baby. I'm glad Ax could be here to take care of you."

I lift my gaze to Dane and strangely enough, I see the same expression on his face as he stares at Lenni. It's plain as day. Adoration and love.

"And I want to wide my bike outside. Ax said you need to say okay. Can I, Mama? Please? I pwomice to wear my helmet."

My brain tries to keep up with her excited chatter. Her face lighting up, she wiggles in his arms and Dane sets her down on the floor again. "Oh, and Mama, I made a picture for you. To make you better. I go show you."

Without any further explanation, she runs out of the room and down the hallway, leaving me under the watchful gaze of Dane. He turns to my bedside table, grabs a glass of water, and hands it to me as I lift my body into a sitting position.

"Here, drink some water. You need to stay hydrated."

I gladly accept the offer and take several long gulps, the cool liquid drenching my parched tongue and dry throat. When I'm finished, he takes the glass from my hand and places it back on the table.

Kneeling beside the bed so we're at eye level, he gives me a grave look of concern.

"You had me worried, Hal. I was about to call in a doctor, you've been so out of it." His eyes flash with what looks like worry. "In fact, if you're okay with it, I want to call my IV therapist to come over. You're in need of some major rehydration."

"Oh. Um, is that necessary? How long have I been out?"

I try to recount the last time I was lucid and aware of what was going on around me. There are flashes of recollection of me lying on the bathroom floor the first night after I put Lenni to bed. The next morning, I remember watching her from my spot on the couch, unable to move a muscle as she poured Cheerios into a bowl, and hearing the cereal pieces scatter over the floor.

I have no memory of texting or talking to Dane.

"Two days," he states. "Three nights."

My mouth drops open, and I gape at him. "Two days? Oh my God. I've never been this sick before."

Dane pats the top of my thighs, still covered in my stinky pajamas. A sudden wave of embarrassment washes over me, and I push his hands away.

"I'm so sorry I burdened you with this. I was…"

"I know, you were desperate." He chuckles and lifts a shoulder. "But look, it's fine. I'm just glad I was in town and could be here for you both. But tomorrow I have to be at a morning practice and I have a game tomorrow night. I'll need to make some arrangements for Lenni."

I wave him off, turning to the side of the mattress and gingerly placing my feet on the floor. I push my palm against his chest to get him to move. "It's fine. I can manage."

He shakes his head when I wobble and then holds me upright with large hands that cup my shoulders. Once I'm stabilized, he then sits down at the edge of the bed next to me.

"Halle, come on. You can barely sit up without passing out, much less take care of Lenni. I can still help you figure it out. I just need to call in some backup and make arrangements. You don't have to do this alone."

Emotion clogs my chest, and I want to burst out in tears. Maybe it's not a wave of dizziness from this virus but a swooning sensation from seeing this side of Dane I've never witnessed before that overtakes me. He's so in control of everything, like all of this is just a walk in the park.

When I don't respond, Dane continues.

"I can drop off Lenni at daycare before practice, and I'll ask Nils Lundren if his nanny can watch Lenni during the game. You just stay here and rest and get yourself better. For both your sakes."

In the past, Dane always played it like he was just an easygoing, cheeky charmer, where everything came easy and the world was his oyster. But he's proven through this to obviously be good under pressure and that he doesn't ruffle easily. Maybe that's what makes him such a good hockey player.

Unlike me. I overthink everything and panic over every decision I make over Lenni.

Even looking for a new pediatrician for Lenni took me over a week to research. I narrowed through the list of doctors, reading through the reviews one by one, creating a spreadsheet of their qualifications and backgrounds before I made my selection.

Even in making the decision to call Dane—although I can't for the life of me remember doing it—I probably stewed over it until I was so sick I could no longer take it.

Before I know I'm saying it, the words slip from my mouth.

"When did you grow up, Dane?"

With a tilt of his head, he quirks an eyebrow and gives me one of his signature smirks, the same one that won me over back in the day. My heart skips a beat.

"I always had it in me, Cherry. I just never had a chance to prove it to you until now."

A noise sounding a lot like a laugh bursts from my lungs, followed by a deep barking cough. "I see you're still full of yourself though, aren't you, hockey boy?"

"When you got both the skills and the looks, Cherry." With a bit of a swagger, he flicks his hand to flip his hair back with a haughty flourish. "Who wouldn't be, eh?"

Oh Mylanta. Dane hasn't changed too much.

But I'll admit, the man may be arrogant and have an ego the size of a hockey arena, but he backs it up with his damn good looks and a level of charm that will steal your heart.

Dane Axelrod is blessed with a fierce jawline that could cut glass and is covered in a tawny honey-colored scruff that makes my fingers want to strum through it. Once again, I'm struck with the physical changes in his body. Toned, muscular arms that look like mountains protruding underneath his form-fitting Henley shirt, and thighs that bulge from years of skating and intense physical workouts that I can't help but yearn to wrap my legs around again.

And he's not just a pretty face, either. Dane has a quick wit and a bold confidence that measures up and makes me swoon.

What he's apparently done with Lenni the past few days while I've been under the weather shows that he is willing to accept fully capable of handling our child.

Which means I need to be even more vigilant at guarding both Lenni's and my hearts.

"Why did you agree to help us?"

Dane's gaze finds mine, his gray eyes flashing with confusion. He grabs my hands in his, and turns my palms face up. His thumbs stroke a lazy pattern over the skin of my wrists and goose bumps of electricity surge through my body.

My sense of smell and taste may be severely affected by this virus, but it doesn't douse the spark of sensual heat I feel from his touch.

"Halle, I would do anything for you." He stares at me from under his long lashes. "And for our daughter."

As if his words summon her, Lenni comes bursting through the bedroom door right on cue. This time, she holds a piece of pink construction paper that she must've pulled out of the cubby in the kitchen.

"Look, Mama! I made a card for you." She shoves the

picture in front of me, and I grab the edge, flipping it around to see the artwork. "And look, Mama, Ax helped me wiff the words and dwaw the hockey stick. He plays hockey like Zack and Drew."

I glance at him and try to hide my smile. And then I look back down at Lenni, who grins broadly with the knowledge she's shared.

"I know, baby. And he's a really good hockey player."

"Yeah. He plays for the Vikings. And he called you baby, too."

My eyes go wide, and I pin him with my question. "Oh? Did he now?"

He shrugs and gives me a wink. "Old habits."

"Yeah. But I towd him you're not a baby. He's silly," she explains, then grabs Dane's hand and pulls his arm. "Come on, Ax. Time to wide my bike."

I watch as my little girl tugs Dane up to his feet and pulls her two-hundred-something-pound father toward the doorway. Dane just looks back at me and grins that boyishly charming smirk.

Oh shit. I'm a goner.

21

Dane

I learned the hard way that a child's car seat does not—and for the record, cannot—fit into the front seat of a Porsche 911 Carrera GTS.

Apparently, car seats must go into the backseat of a car. Who knew?

Lenni did.

She expertly explained to me in no uncertain terms that "You can't do that, silly. Kids sit in the back." I may have covertly googled that safety tip after her pronouncement, not extremely confident in the words of a four-year-old.

But sure enough, what she said was indeed accurate. The site I found said that kids had to sit in the back seat and remain in forward-facing child safety seats until the age of seven, switching to booster seats until they reach a specific maximum height and weight. Jesus, how do parents know this stuff?

Are there playbooks for raising kids? If so, I need to get one pronto.

It's a strange off-kilter feeling to not know what to do, and it has my confidence level plummeting. Give me a question about hockey, and I'll give you the answer before you can spit. But a kid? I feel dumber than a box of rocks.

Not only did the car seat thing throw me for a loop this morning sending me behind schedule, but so did the tantrum Lenni had over not wanting to remove her pajamas and put on clothes for school.

I may have bribed her with candy. Not my finest moment, but again, novice here. I used what tools I had at my disposal to take down my opponent and win the game.

But now I'm stuck rooting around the kitchen in search of Halle's car keys so I can drive her car that's correctly car seat-equipped. I've looked in all the usual places where I'd place a set of keys. They aren't in a kitchen drawer. Or on a hook. Or even on a hallway table.

"Hey Lulu Lennon, do you know where your mommy keeps her car keys?"

Halle had fallen back to sleep about an hour ago, after I'd brought her some juice and toast and then helped make sure she was fine on her own in the bathroom. She seemed less wobbly then, but I still had no intention of walking back in there to wake her up with a question when I'm sure I can find the keys on my own. I am bound and determined to handle this situation without her assistance.

Lenni sits at the kitchen table finishing the bowl of gummy worms I gave her to placate her while I changed her into a kid-approved outfit.

She turns her head to look at me over her shoulder and gives me that face, the one that says *you're an idiot*.

"In her purse."

"Um, okay. Do you know where she might have put that, Miss Smarty Pants?" I close the kitchen drawer I was rifling through and do a quick scan around the floor by the front door and couch to see if maybe I missed it somewhere.

Lenni giggles and shoves more gummies in her mouth, muffling her answer. "Nope."

I ruffle her hair as I walk by. Another part of her earlier meltdown was because she wanted me to put her hair in braids. Braids? Not a chance. She was lucky I managed to get a brush through her hair, which is still a wild, matted mess and looks like she went through a wind tunnel.

"Okay. Well, stay right here and I'll go find them so we can get going."

I check my watch and grumble. I am going to get hell for being late to practice. While Halle was in the bathroom earlier, I'd already sent a text to Coach T to let him know there was a chance I might be late due to an "unexpected family emergency." And before she fell back asleep, Halle sent off a message to her boss informing him she was still sick at home. Then she called Lenni's teacher at Little Vikings daycare to grant permission and consent for me to drop Lenni off and pick her up today and possibly tomorrow.

If the teacher thought that was strange, she didn't remark on it. She also didn't ask my relation to Lenni, and Halle made no mention that I am Lennon's dad. She simply stated I was a friend of the family and assisting with Lenni while she was under the weather.

I'm not going to lie. My feelings were low-key hurt that my fatherly duties seemed to have an expiration date stamped on them. But I'm not going to let it get me down. I have faith that she'll come around once she sees how far I've come just in the past few days. During this time, I've had a crash course in childcare, learning through the educational lens of a four-year-old exactly how to do things.

The first, of course, and most important, is how to properly play make-believe and pretend to be Olaf. Had to google that one, too. I was also instructed on how to make the perfect pancakes and pour the appropriate amount of syrup over them. Pretty sure it was more than one child should ever consume in one breakfast. And there was the lesson on how to gently glide a brush through bedhead hair without snagging it through all the snarls. I did not, however, master a ponytail. Why do they make those twist-ties so damn tiny?

And lastly, I've learned just how very difficult it is to

get an extremely energetic little girl to bed. For the record, it took close to ten thousand books and a made-up song I sung off key for her to finally close her eyes and fall asleep.

The question that flits through my mind is how the hell does Halle handle this every single day?

I swear to God, I think it's harder to raise a child than it is to attend training camp every year.

My feet pad quietly down the hallway toward Halle's back bedroom. I'd left the door slightly ajar when she went back to bed in case she needed something. When I approach, the light in the room is still off, so I quietly place my palm on the door and push it open, hoping to step quietly inside in search of Halle's purse.

But that's not what happens.

Instead of a purse, I find Halle standing in the middle of the room, completely naked and facing directly toward the door as I tiptoe into her room.

She shrieks, one arm flying out to cover her naked breasts and the other dipping lower to hide the area between her legs—but not before I get an eyeful of her in her birthday suit.

"What the hell, Dane? Don't you knock?"

Obviously, I've seen naked women before. And she is one of them. I've had a lot of firsthand experience with how perfectly supple her tits are. My hands and mouth have explored that soft, plump terrain, and those memories are still often featured in my dreams.

My gaze flashes with interest as I descend over her

form. The fuller curves of her hips and stomach, and the smooth skin of her slightly parted thighs.

Shit. I'm staring, and I know I shouldn't, but I can't seem to move my feet to turn away.

"Get out!"

"Sorry... sorry..." I mumble, yanking my eyes away from her, albeit a little reluctantly, and pivoting quickly to face the open doorway. I'm about to leave the room when I remember through my haze that I came in for a valid reason, and it wasn't to stare at Halle's body. That was an unfortunate but not unwelcome surprise on my part. "I need your keys."

"My what?" There's a rustle of clothing from behind me.

Out of the corner of my peripheral, I can see movement as Halle shoves her hands in an oversized T-shirt.

"I can't find your car keys. I need them so Lenni and I can leave."

"Oh... yeah, okay. They're in my purse."

I chuckle. "Yeah, I know that part. That's why I'm in here."

"Okay, I'm good. You can turn around now."

I move much more cautiously this time, slowly turning in a half-circle and shoving my hands in my pockets. Halle is now bent over and rooting around the floor, tossing clothing around in search of her purse.

The only problem with her current state of attire is that her oversized shirt does not cover an important— and gorgeous—feature she possesses. The way she's bent over gives me an unobstructed view of her curvy ass clad in a pair of pink panties.

And now I know she's trying to kill me.

I exhale and turn to look at the unmade bed.

But fuck, that doesn't do me any good either because now I'm thinking about Halle naked... in bed.

I can't win.

"I want you to know I'm usually very organized and tidy. I don't live like this at all," she says, gesturing toward her room. Then she unearths a bag that looks more like a suitcase than a purse. "Found it!"

She stands back up, holding it in the air, and my torture has mercifully come to an end. It won't, however, be the last time I think about Halle naked. That visual will be stuck in my head for days, possibly weeks to come.

While I watch her dig inside the giant purse, I wonder if she'll be okay without me around today.

"Hey, Halle. Are you sure you don't need me to call in some help while I'm gone?"

A jingle of keys announces the lost has now been found and she smiles. It's the first one I've seen in days, and even through the lens of illness, her smile can still dazzle me stupid.

She places the key ring in the palm of my outstretched hand. I expect her to just drop them in, but instead, she clutches the keys and my hand and squeezes.

Our eyes connect. Despite the dark circles and red, swollen eyes, I see her more clearly than I ever have before.

She is incandescent and as authentic as they come. I'm literally in awe of who she has become in the face of everything these past five years. She brought a child into this world and raised her, all while I've been living free and having fun.

Halle has proven that she is driven, ambitious, and also a great mother to her daughter.

"I can't ever repay you, Dane," she sniffles. "I'm so sorry I never…"

I cut her off when I pull her into me, pressing her body against my chest and wrapping her in my arms.

"I would do it again a hundred times over," I whisper into her hair, placing a kiss on top of her head. "She's my daughter. I did it for you both."

When I release her from my hold, she steps back, sniffles, and lowers her head to stare at the floor. I cup her cheek and lift her chin to meet my gaze.

"I loved getting to know her, Halle. She's such a great kid. And I hope once you're feeling better, we can sit down and talk through the hard stuff, like when we can tell her I'm her dad."

On that note, I turn and stride out of the room, readying myself for my first preschool drop-off.

It's scarier than heading into Game 7 of the Cup finals.

22

———

Halle

It's been so long since I've had an entire eight hours of alone time, I don't even know what to do with myself.

Now that the fog has lifted, I have strength to take a shower, do my laundry, and pick this place up. I head into the bathroom and turn on the faucet, waiting for the old pipes to warm the water up. Washing off the gross stink that's collected on me while I've been in my sickbed is priority number one.

As I wait for the water to heat, I make the mistake of glancing into the bathroom mirror and nearly jump back at my reflection. I look like I'm in a *Walking Dead* episode.

My God, it's horrifying.

My hair is jumbled, unkempt chaos, pushed halfway in and out of a bun I finally shoved it into this morning. After days of sweaty fever sleep, it's in desperate need of a wash. Leaning into the mirror for a closer examination of my face, I'm shocked to see how bedraggled I look. Bluish bags cling under my puffy red eyes, and my sallow skin makes me appear to have been dug up from a shallow grave.

I shudder at the sight of my zombie-like appearance and yank off my robe and the T-shirt I'd hastily thrown on after Dane caught me naked by surprise. I toss them in the hamper and stand in front of the mirror, then critically examine my body, trying to see what Dane must have. My fingertips explore the skin along my collarbone, and I remember the way Dane froze in my doorway when he walked in and then didn't turn away.

It was unexpected—and dare I say, thrilling—to have his eyes roam over my nakedness in that sensual way a lover's gaze does. My hand drops to my left breast, dreamily stroking my nipple with my thumb, the sensitive nub stiffening under the caressing touch.

It's been so long since I've been touched. I wonder what it would've been like had Dane stepped closer, cupped my breasts in his palms, seeking and finding all my erogenous spots. My own hand glides down over my belly—the stomach that was once flat and firm but now is soft, with a slight belly pooch from bearing a child. I run my hand over the curve of my hips and then slip my fingers between my legs, a soft moan escaping my lips as I drag them through the wetness of my folds and circle the sensitive nub.

Closing my eyes from the sensation that overtakes

me, I reach out a hand to grip the edge of the counter and allow the image of Dane to come to the forefront of my mind. I imagine him kneeling in front of me, rough hands grasping my curvy hips, face between my thighs as he pushes his wet tongue at my entrance.

The orgasm comes out of nowhere with surprising force, like a ten-foot cresting wave hitting the sand. My head drops forward, and I exhale a shaky breath. My body feels limp from pleasure, yet I still feel empty and lonely.

When I return to myself, I stare once again at my reflection and let out a short laugh. Nearly twenty-five years old, a single mom and a recent college grad, and I've only ever had one man inside me.

Dane.

It's embarrassing to admit, but my love life has been a nonexistent priority. Raising my daughter and getting through my online college program was always my focus. I had to make something of myself so I could be an example for Lenni.

It was hard work, and sometimes I felt defeated on those nights when she wouldn't sleep or was fussy, but never once did I regret having Lenni. She's my North Star.

But one thing I may be regretting is whether I've made the right decision to keep Dane in the dark all those years. Seeing him with her and watching the way he's stepped in to handle things while I've been sick makes me question what I should do now.

He still wants an answer about when we can tell Lenni that he's her dad.

I weigh the options as I step into the tub, ducking under the hot stream of water. I luxuriate in the scent of my body wash and the heat of the deluge, washing away all the unpleasantness of illness. My soapy hands move over my body, recognizing all the changes since giving birth.

The last time I was with Dane, I was in the best shape of my life. I was firm and fit from playing volleyball, and, let's be honest, I was also in an eighteen-year-old body. Now I'm a woman with C-cup boobs, hips that have stretched and widened, and thighs that no longer fit into the skinny jeans of my past. And my ass—Lord help me, but you could say it has a postal code all its own.

With a heavy sigh, I step out of the tub and reach for a towel when I hear my phone chirping from a distance. A strange thrill zings through me pebbling my flesh as I wonder if it's Dane.

Wrapping the towel around me, I rush into the bedroom and peer down at the notification on the screen. It's an email from Trevor, possibly in response to my earlier email.

My stomach sinks, and a new seed of concern blooms in my head.

What if he fires me? I've already been out far more days than any new employee should be when they are barely a month on the job. Trevor must think I'm a lazy, unreliable employee who just wants to sit around and use up personal days.

It kills me that he might think I'm not doing my job. The reality is, kids get sick, and I thought moms are supposed to be immune and invincible.

That's not my luck.

I send a silent prayer up to the universe and open my email app. With a shaky finger, I click on the message.

Hey Halle.

Got your message and I'm just checking in on how you're doing. I ran into Ax this morning down in the staff wing. He said you were very ill and needed more time to recover. That is absolutely no problem. I'd prefer you stay at home when sick, anyway. Better to keep your sick germs to yourself and not spread it to your colleagues. Ha Ha

I hope that doesn't sound insensitive because I am truly worried about you. The flu bug this year is a rough one. Please take all the time you need to recover.

However, if you're bored and only when you feel up to it, you have my permission to work remotely when needed. But for now, please don't worry about a thing here.

With that, I hope you get some rest. The team has it covered for you.
See you soon. Be well.
Trevor

Oh my God. Could I be any more humiliated that Dane shared the status of my health with Trevor?

I can't imagine what opinion Trevor has already formed about me this week.

H. E. Double Hockey Sticks.

This is exactly what I don't want. I want to bury my head in my pillows and scream. I would, too, but I haven't washed them yet.

I need to fix this, and quick.

I respond with a note thanking him for his care and generosity and then let him know I'm on the mend and will do a complete review of the reports on my task list later this evening.

Once I'm done with that, I change into a pair of leggings and an oversized sweatshirt, strip the sheets, start the laundry, and crash on my couch. The energy I'd had after my shower has dwindled, and I expended more than I had in the tank. That's the hard part of recovering. You feel good until you don't any longer.

Being sick sucks, especially when you have no one to take care of you.

My head snaps up when I hear the front door unlock and it flies open as Dane glides in like he's still wearing skates, carrying a bag of something that smells warm and delicious.

"Oh good, you're up. Ready for some lunch?"

He floats in like a figment of my imagination, and heads directly toward the kitchen. I sit, dumbfounded, and watch as he enthusiastically opens and closes cabinet doors, taking out plates and utensils to clearly indicate he's made himself at home in my house.

This man is unbelievable. Who is he? Who has he become?

Dane Axelrod isn't the same great guy I used to know.

I think he might just be better.

23

D ane

"I'll tell you what. I think I had a crash course on four-year-olds this week," I say over a mouthful of food.

I was starving after practice and had stopped in at Louie's for takeaway, picking up some soup and a turkey sandwich for Halle in the hopes she would be hungry and up to eating. And I was worried she might need something, so I wanted to swing by to check on her anyway. "I didn't know what I didn't know, ya know?" I took another bite of my toasted club sandwich.

She laughs and nods. "Oh, I know all right."

"She's a chatterbox, that one. I can't imagine who she gets that from." I give Halle a pointed look.

From the other end of the couch where she sits, she lifts a brow of disagreement, a smile turning up at the corners of her mouth. I could tell by the glow of her fresh-faced smile when I walked in the door, and the damp strands of hair braided through her thick auburn hair that she'd taken a shower while I was gone. She also is dressed casually in a pair of black leggings that hug all those new and generous curves of hers, and a light gray sweatshirt that gives the barest hint of her shoulder. My fingers twitch to run over the smooth slope of skin, and I kind of miss the T-shirt and panties.

Being in Halle's presence without a small kid close by is an unusual place to find myself. It's also confusing to be on a couch with a beautiful woman and not try to make the moves to get her naked.

While Halle and I know each other intimately, the space between us is cluttered with so much of the past, I don't know how I should act around her now. What I would've done on this couch with her five years ago is a completely different vibe than now.

Plus, we have things left to resolve.

"Lenni is a master storyteller,"she agrees, bringing the spoon to her mouth as I stare at her lips. She looks up from her spoon, and our eyes connect. She quirks a brow. "What else did you learn?"

I wipe a napkin over the cleft in my chin, worried I have mustard stuck in my beard, and consider her question.

"Well, she's pretty opinionated and kind of a know-it-all." My lips curl upward at the corners. "She obviously got that trait from you."

The sound of Halle's laughter bouncing around the

room is a gift from the universe and lights me up from head to toe. It'll remain on my life soundtrack for as long as I live.

"You are so full of shit," she argues, tossing her balled-up napkin at me. "I'm not opinionated in the slightest."

"That's exactly what you would say." I blow a raspberry and then snap my fingers. "Oh, and another thing. Lenni is stubborn as a goat. And I don't mean the greatest of all time. That kid dug her heels in yesterday morning until I made pancakes." I make a face, tightening my lips together. "I didn't realize kids that age could have such meltdowns and use them to negotiate. She got her pancakes."

Another laugh and the corners of her eyes crinkle, eyes sparkling with amusement. "Yeah, kids that age are learning to express themselves and don't have a grasp on their emotions quite yet. So, the big feelings often come out in a tantrum."

I chuckle. "I know a few hockey players who do that, too."

She smiles and brings her glass of juice to her lips, taking a dainty sip. I watch the movement of her delicate throat as she swallows. When she tilts her head back, I turn away. It's sensory overload to be on this couch with her, to watch her laugh and listen to her speak but be unable to touch her the way I want.

Not the way I used to. If I'm not careful, it might just be me having a tantrum if I don't put some distance between us. I reach forward and set my empty plate on the sofa table, covertly adjusting myself in my pants.

It's good to see that Halle is feeling better and seems to have regained her strength. The fact that she soon won't need me to stick around bums me out. I didn't know how much I'd enjoy being the guy who can be counted on to take care of things. I'd never envisioned myself in the role of caretaker or what it would be like to be in dad mode.

But hanging out and playing with Lenni was an eye-opening experience for me. It was fun and challenging, and gave me a deeper respect for Halle. For parents in general.

And spending this time with her—just sitting together and enjoying the easy companionship we have —makes me realize how much I've missed it. How much I've missed her. The conversation and teasing banter have flowed as if we've never been apart.

Since Halle's reappearance in my life, I've been reminiscing a lot about our past. To others, it may have been barely enough time to get to know someone, but a connection was forged back then, and we've picked up where we left off.

It sounds so cliché to say out loud, but maybe it's a cosmic soulmate thing or some crazy shit like that.

I may not believe in that stuff, but I do know that Halle does something to me that no other woman has ever done. She stirs me from the inside out—lights my soul on fire, like the flames of a torch—and makes me want more.

That desire is more than physical attraction, but it's a strong urge I have to fight every time she's close. When we were together in the past, my hands were always touching her. Holding hands, kissing her neck, stroking her back, nipping my lips over her skin.

When it comes to Halle, it's as if we are bound by a tether that stretched and pulled but never broke.

Is it possible that strong feelings like I had for her don't ever fully disappear? They just resurface bigger than before?

"So, besides this bout with the flu, how are you both adjusting to life in Vancouver?" I ask, throwing an arm on the back of the couch, resisting the urge to run a hand over the braid that's inches from my fingers. I clutch the cushion with a firm grasp to keep myself from stroking her silky auburn locks.

Halle pauses for a moment, the deep groove lines between her brows pinching together as she considers my question. When our eyes meet, hers glisten with tears. A droplet hangs on her lashes, and I reach out and swipe it away with my thumb before it can drop.

She blinks and then sniffles. I grab a tissue from the box and hand it to her as tears gush from the corners of her eyes. "I'm not going to lie. It's been so hard."

"Oh, baby, don't do that to yourself." I wrap my arm around her shoulders, pulling her into my body and tucking her into my chest. Her slight body is racked with sobs. "Shh. It's okay. You're going to be okay. I promise."

She quiets after a few moments as I continue to rub small circles over her back, consoling her the only way I know how.

"It's stupid, because she's been gone so long, but there are times it hurts so bad that I can't call my mother to ask her advice." Her voice is mournful and it breaks my heart. If there was something I could do to fix it, I would. "It makes me feel guilty, too, like I'm betraying my dad by wanting her. He's done so much for us, but it's not the same as having a mom."

I glide a hand over her head in calming strokes. Halle's situation is way outside my knowledge base, and honestly, I don't know if giving my opinion will make it better or worse. So, I listen and comfort as she talks.

"It's going on nearly ten years, but I miss here every day. There are times—so many times—when I don't know what I'm doing, and another mother would help. Not having that in my life right now... it's so lonely." Her shoulders rise and fall in jerky movements as she hiccups through the words.

Halle remains cocooned in my embrace for several minutes as I try to come up with something brilliant to say in response.

"You can always call my mom," I offer, tipping my head down so I can see her face. "I bet she'd love to give you advice. She's always trying to tell me what to do."

A loud snort belts out from Halle's lungs, and she

presses her palms against my chest, pushing herself upright.

"Right. I'm sure she'd totally be open to hearing from some random stranger about dealing with raising a kid, especially how to get one back to sleep after she wakes up at three a.m. and wants to play."

My nose wrinkles. "Whoa. Does that happen regularly?"

"Every single night." She sighs heavily, the fatigue evident.

"I'm pretty sure she slept through the nights I've been here," I say, smiling confidently. She raises a skeptical brow.

It is an absolute fact that Lenni had me spinning my wheels and jumping through hoops like a trained circus pony at bedtime. Every night, from beginning to end, it took me no less than an hour and a half until she closed her eyes and finally fell asleep. There were books to read, drinks of water to fetch, potty time, story time, checking for monsters under the bed. You name it, Lenni was sure to make it happen.

When I would finally close her bedroom door, I would come out to the living room, plop down on the couch with the TV turned on to hockey highlights, and fall asleep instantly.

Halle gives me a shrewd look, and my eyes grow wide, my mouth gaping open. "Wait, what? She woke up? How did I not know that?"

"You were sound asleep out here. Snoring loudly, I might

add." She laughs with a shrug. "Thankfully, you wore her out enough for her to go back down without too much work."

"Ah, shit, Hal. I'm so sorry you were disturbed." I offer an apologetic smile and lay a hand on her knee. "Here I was, feeling like hot shit, when instead, I literally fell asleep on the job. I'll be better tonight."

Halle shakes her head and scoots away, creating additional distance between us. I miss the heat of her snuggled next to me.

"Honestly, now that I'm back in the land of the living and you have your game, I think we'll be fine without you. I can take care of my own daught—" She stops suddenly, the corners of her mouth turning into a frown, her brows furrowing together. "I meant..."

"It's all good. I've only been in her life a short time, and, well, you've been her mother from the start." I take her hands in mine, gazing into her eyes hopefully. "I'd love it if you give me a chance with her."

And you.

I don't have a chance to say that because my phone vibrates in my pocket with an incoming call. I let go of her hands and root around in the front of my jeans, extracting it to check the display.

"Oh shit," I grumble, realizing exactly what the call is about. "It's the team's PR rep. I need to take this."

"Of course. I'll go grab some more tea in the kitchen."

"Hello?" I answer, my gaze following Halle's backside as she walks toward the other room. Damn, her ass looks amazing in those leggings, round and firm globes accentuated by toned legs. What I wouldn't give to dig my fingers in the curves of her hips and feel her legs locked around my waist.

For a second, I get lost in a memory until the voice of Nat Stinson, our PR coordinator, shakes me free.

"Dane, it's Nat. You didn't forget about the video podcast interview we scheduled for you with Jones Hartley today, did you?"

I make a face and check my calendar app. Sure enough, there it is. I'd promised Ballas I'd do this interview, but I completely forgot it was today.

"Yeah, yeah, yeah, of course I didn't forget." Halle watches me and I cross one finger over the other. "Yep, I'm on my way, just had an errand to run. See you in a bit."

I disconnect the call and jump off the couch, feeling the weight of Halle's stare from across the room. She stands in the middle of the kitchen holding a mug of tea with both hands, the steam rising and curling around her face. Her eyebrows are lifted to the ceiling.

"Gotta go?" she asks, the tone light and without censure.

I sweep up my keys from the coffee table and realize I've left a mess for her to clean up. "Yeah. Shit, I forgot I about this publicity thing before the game." I snap my fingers as another thing dawns on me. "That reminds me... Lenni's pickup after daycare is all squared away today. I'll be there to get her, and Lundy's wife, Helena, will drive her home and drop her off with you."

Halle's shoulders slump, and she drops her chin to her chest. "Oh, how embarrassing, Dane. You shouldn't have had to enlist someone I don't know to help me out."

I step toward her with a grin, bopping her on the tip of her button nose. She stubbornly jerks her head away.

"It takes a village, Cherry." I wink and flash her my signature smile. "So, get used to the extra help because you and Lenni are part of the Vikings family now."

24

___

Halle

After Dane left my house, he sent me Helena Lundren's contact information so we could arrange a time for Lenni's drop-off. I'm not sure what I expect from Helena, but it isn't such a gracious and helpful woman.

I had spent the afternoon cleaning up around the house. I'll hand it to Dane, he did his best at keeping things neat, but I still found cereal bits under my couch and Lenni's toothbrush hidden in her toy castle.

After the last dish is put away, I scan my house and try view it from the perspective of a woman who probably lives in a lavishly decorated multimillion-dollar home with expensive furniture and décor. My small, two-bedroom, mid-century-style home, while tastefully decorated, is a humble rental with cheap Ikea and estate sale furnishings.

I remind myself that this is my first place of my own and it's filled with love, which I think is the most important aspect of a home.

The doorbell finally rings at four forty-five, and I rush to open the door, having missed my sweet girl. As soon as it swings open, there's a whoosh of pigtails and a flash of movement when Lenni and another little girl fly past me like a flock of birds, squawking as they dash inside hand in hand.

"Hi, Mama!" Lenni calls out as she and the towheaded girl run to the area where I just arranged all her toys. "This is Elise. We're gonna play pwincesses!"

Her excitement is a tangible gift and fills me with pride. In the short time we've been in Vancouver, and she's attended the daycare, Lenni has blossomed from clingy to independent and more social. The transformation has been remarkable. It soothes my constant guilt over whether this move was the right choice for us.

Based on the changes my daughter has exhibited, it was a good decision.

Apparently, she didn't get those sociable traits from me. I awkwardly stand in the doorway as Helena holds the handle of a baby carrier with one hand and waits to be invited in.

"Where are my manners? Please, come inside and have a seat," I offer, gesturing to my living room couch. "And hello, by the way. I'm Halle MacAlister."

The tall, slim, woman with model looks smiles brightly and walks toward the couch, gingerly setting the carrier down on the floor next to it. A blanket extends over the opening so I can't get a peek at the baby yet, but the child is obviously sleeping.

"Nice to meet you, Halle," Helena says with a hint of a Scandinavian accent, and takes a seat on my blue fabric couch with perfect posture and grace. I'm not sure how old the baby is, but you'd never know by looking at Helena that she's had one child, let alone two. "And that's my oldest, Elise, who just ran past. This sleeping beauty is Ingrid."

She lifts off the blanket so I can peer inside at one of the most beautiful babies I've ever seen, with a rosy-cheeked face and a nearly bald head sporting just a tuft of white-blond hair on the top.

My hand covers my heart. "Oh, what an angel. She's beautiful. How old? About nine or ten months?"

Helena removes the pacifier from Ingrid's chest, where it must have popped out of the sleeping baby's mouth, and loops her finger through the ring.

"Thirteen months next week. Ingrid's much more chunk than length at this point." Her laughter is like the sound of carol bells ringing, light and airy. "And Elise is three and a half."

I sigh, glancing over to where the girls play with Lenni's dolls, and then return my attention to Ingrid, whom I itch to pick up and snuggle. "I really miss the baby stage sometimes."

Helena gives me a pointed look, her crystal blue eyes

sparkling. "I bet you don't miss the sleepless nights or dirty diapers though."

"Touche," I agree with a smile, sparing a look at the girls. "It's nice now that Lenni is four and can do a lot of things on her own, like go to the bathroom at home by herself."

"That's one of the reasons I waited until Elise was walking and talking before getting pregnant again."

My gaze falls again to the flat of her stomach and then the gigantic diamond ring on her finger. I'm envious that, as a married mother, she probably had the opportunity to plan out her pregnancies with her partner and decide when to add to their family.

Unlike me, who didn't have the chance and may never have another opportunity to have another child. That would require a man, which I do not have.

"Oh my gosh, I haven't even offered you or the girls anything to eat or drink. Can I get you something? Water? Juice? Tea?"

"Vodka?" she says with a breezy laugh. I search her clear blue eyes and determine she's joking. But I do notice the darkened circles underneath her eyes, an indicator of those sleepless nights I remember so well.

With the season in full swing, and a young baby to boot, Helena likely does most of the parenting without much assistance from her hockey player husband. It increases my level of guilt even more that she was dragged into this huge favor.

When I don't answer immediately, she reaches out and pats my arm.

"I'm kidding," she clarifies, lifting an expressive brow. "I'm not much of a drinker anyway, but it's been one hellish week. The baby is colicky, Elise has been cranky, and the boys go out on the road again tomorrow. Hockey season is exhausting with two littles."

I want to agree with her but honestly, life is always exhausting as a single mom with no one but myself to rely on.

"I hear ya."

It's the reason I don't want to rely on Dane to help me out. While I am so grateful for his help these last few days, he won't always be around. He could be here one day and gone the next.

Isn't that the sort of guy he is? Quick to leave and not look back?

"I can only imagine the chaos his schedule causes. I hope you at least have some nanny coverage to help?" I ask, moving into the kitchen connected to the living room. It's an open concept, which I love, because I can easily keep an eye on Lenni while cooking and preparing meals.

The baby starts to fuss, and I watch Helena soothe her with a soft coo, inserting the pacifier back in Ingrid's mouth.

"Yes, Greta is our live-in au pair. She's the second one we've had this year, and so far, she's working out great. She helps me with the girls and basic chores when Nils is gone or when I need a break to run errands or whatever," she explains. I stare dreamily at her, wondering what it would be like to have a break. "But it's also weird to have someone else living in your space. You know what I mean?"

Not really.

Pulling two coffee mugs down from a cabinet shelf, I say, "I don't know what you want to drink, but I have a Keurig. You could have some very strong coffee—with or without the booze. You choose." I wink, and it draws out an elegant laugh from her mouth.

As I prepare the drinks, I notice Helena scanning the room, taking in my home. It feels like she's searching for something, some kind of inside scoop about our lives.

"Helena, I want to thank you again for helping me with Lenni today. You obviously have enough on your plate, and I feel awful you had to get involved. But Dane was adamant I stay home and rest."

She swings her gaze back to me, her blond ponytail flipping over her shoulder, and she taps her fingers on her chin.

"Speaking of involved—and please forgive me, but no one has ever considered me tactful—are you and Dane together?"

The spoon in my hand slips from my fingers and clatters to the floor, bouncing off the wood floor and splattering creamer on my leggings.

"Buckets," I curse, avoiding a real swear word in case the girls are listening. I kneel down to pick up the spoon and dab away the droplets that paint my leg like abstract art. I take the time to consider the best way to answer that.

I mean, Dane and I are not *together* together. We have a shared past and a shared child now, so *involved* is one way to explain our relationship. No one else knows about that second aspect of our connection, and I don't know enough about Helena to divulge that secret.

When I stand back up, I paste on what I hope is an honest smile.

"I like a woman who gets to the point and doesn't beat around the bush," I acknowledge as Helena moves toward me and stops at the other end of the island. I hand her the hot mug of coffee and a clean spoon to use.

She accepts the mug and immediately places it down on the counter before leaning forward in a conspiratorial fashion.

I shake my head, uncertain how to respond. "Dane and I have history, but we're not together now. We're just friends."

She cocks her head to the side and pins me with a skeptical look.

"Just friends... hmm." She cups her delicate chin in her palm, planting her elbow on the countertop. "That's interesting because I've known Dane for a while now, and I've never known him to be 'just friends' with a woman. And I've never witnessed this side of him."

I can't help myself. "What side is that?"

She chuckles. "The side where he goes out of his way

to help a woman and her child. Unless, that is, there's some benefit in it for him. Wink. Wink."

I stir some creamer in my cup and worry my lip.

"I'm sure I don't know what you mean," I say, using an innocent tone. "But I promise, there are no benefits being had."

"Hmm... not yet anyhow." She waggles her perfectly shaped brows. "But it's clear you're someone very special to him."

With each additional question she asks, Helena uncovers more of the story, getting closer and closer to the truth. I need to find a way to steer this ship in another direction and quick.

"So how did you and Nils meet?"

Helena takes a sip of her coffee, her bright eyes and eyebrows softening in understanding. "Okay, I get it... change of subject matter. Point taken. I'll butt out." She sets her coffee back on the counter and lifts both hands in the air. "I won't pry anymore. At least, not until you want to share. Then watch out."

She grins broadly, extending her hand to pat the top of mine. We both glance over to the girls, who are now dancing along to a Taylor Swift song.

"I'm sorry, I know I come on so strong," Helena says. "I've just moved so much with Nils that I don't waste time anymore with the subtleties when developing friendships."

I laugh. "You're fine. And you didn't waste any time in coming to our aid today. I want you to know I will return the favor anytime you need it. That's what friends are for."

Helena squeezes my mind.

Her crystal blue eyes sparkle. "Establishing meaningful local female friendships as hockey wives can be difficult. If we do find friends, we're forced to leave them behind the minute our partners get traded."

Her sentiments convey exactly my concern over letting Dane get close to Lenni. My worst fear is that she learns that Dane is her dad, she gets attached to him, and he gets traded, leaves her behind, and becomes an absent father.

"I'm sure that's really hard to manage, especially with two young kids."

"Which is precisely why I'm so glad to have another WAG with a child. Most of the other players' partners are young and still into clubbing every night." She waves a dismissive hand in the air. "Not to imply you're old, but at least you and I can get the girls together and have playdates."

As if on cue, the girls squeal in playful delight, drawing our attention over to the living room. They are happy and content with each other, and my heart expands with the knowledge we've both made new friends.

"Absolutely. Just one correction, though. I'm not a WAG; I only work for the team."

Helena snickers. "If you say so."

25

———

Dane

"Helena mentioned both she and Elise had a great time with Halle and Lennon today," Nils says in his typical low-key, no-nonsense tone as we hit the locker room post-game.

We're celebrating a big W tonight against Boston, zipping it up in the final period, two to zero. Both of our team goals were scored by Thorny, with his first goal made straight off the faceoff not even twenty seconds into the game. It was a glorious play, with an easy-breezy flip of the puck into the net around the goalie's stick.

The second goal was an assist from me to Thorny. I set it up with a quick pass from the right, with a double screen in front of the net by Rossco and Lyons. Oli let go of a bomb from up top, the perfect laser goal that kept us in the lead the entire game.

We're still early in the season, but the more Ws we

can stack up, the better. It feels like this year our team is really gelling like no other. We have some strong, key players—me included—and no one is out for his own glory. It's truly a team effort.

I scrub a towel over my wet hair and turn toward Nils with a grin.

"Yeah, those two are easy to like, man. And thank Helena again for doing me that solid. That was cool of her." I cast him a glance. "Especially after that thing with her sister."

A few months ago, right around the playoffs and through the beginning of our summer, Helena's younger sister, Karolina, came over from Norway to visit the family. She'd of course attended a few of our end-of-season games and we ended up meeting one night at a post-game party held over at Brewer's house.

One thing led to another, and Karolina wound up coming home with me. We had a fantastic night together. The next morning, however, Karolina started making plans for us to hang out again during her trip, which was not on my agenda. I'd made it clear from the beginning that our hookup was a one-time thing, and she wasn't happy with me when I hurriedly ushered her out of the house, wishing her a good rest of her visit.

Based on the looks I now get from Helena, she must have heard a different story from her sister and I get the feeling she formed an unfavorable opinion about me after that.

The thing that confused me was how Karolina could

have misunderstood my intentions. I'm not a guy who toys with women's hearts. I may not be high on the emotional intelligence scale—something my younger sister, a business psychology major, has accused me of before—but I'm not an asshole who aims at hurting a woman.

I always try to let women know my rules from the very beginning. The rules are there to ensure we both had a good time together—preferably naked—and then go our merry ways. To help keep feelings from getting mixed up and entangled together. No tears of goodbye. No frustration and fights when a call or text doesn't come through after a long road trip. And absolutely zero emotions.

I pull on a clean shirt over my head, tug a pair of jeans up my legs, and tuck the T-shirt hem into my waistband. Then I run a hand through damp hair and turn to notice Nils is ready to go. He throws his used towels in the bin at the end of the bench and stares at me like he's trying to figure me out.

"You going to tell me about your involvement with this woman and her kid?"

Something flares to life inside me—a protective instinct over my connection with Halle and Lenni. Unfortunately, Halle doesn't want this out in the open yet. While I respect her reservations even though I don't completely understand the reasons for them, I'm not at liberty to spill the tea to anyone right now. I promised

Halle, for Lenni's sake, to not let it slip that I'm her biological father.

Until Lennon knows the truth, it can't be shared publicly.

Putting on my poker face, I keep my tone casual and give the same spiel I've given everyone else, hoping he can't read through me.

"I've known Halle since I played in juniors. She just moved here for the job as one of the team's analysts, so she doesn't really know anyone, and asked for my help. So, I helped." I shrug a shoulder nonchalantly.

Nils rubs his bearded chin and stares at me with an assessing gaze.

"Hmm... okay. Just seems out of character for you."

I wrinkle my nose at his shade. I may sleep around a lot, but that doesn't mean I won't step out on a limb to help my friends.

"Dude, I'm not a total self-centered prick. She's my friend and needed my help. End of story."

Nils lets out a disbelieving snicker, one brow quirked skyward. "Sure, Ax. Go ahead and tell yourself that." He levels me with his blue eyes. "I know how you operate. You don't do friends with a woman. It's impossible."

He's not wrong. I probably couldn't name one unless I go back in time to the second grade. I've had girls' attention almost all my life and it gained momentum when I started playing hockey. Hockey players are viewed as hometown heroes in Canada. Right or wrong, we wear badges of honor for being athletic and good at the sport.

Let's face it, that level of admiration has a profound impact on one's inflated self-esteem.

Ergo, my ego.

"Just because you've never seen me with a female friend—" I use air quotes and twist my face—"doesn't mean I haven't had one. Have you been friends with a woman before, Lundy?"

I turn the tables as we walk side by side out the locker room, carrying our bags slung over our shoulders.

"Yeah, my wife was my best childhood friend." He gives me a pointed sideways look. "Which proves my point. Don't kid yourself. Your friendship with Halle is doomed to be shut down by your dick."

I'm saved by the bell from discussing this any further when Rossco approaches us from behind, slapping his oversized mitts on each of our shoulders.

"Who's Halle?" he asks in a sly tone. "And is she hot and up for a threesome?"

I slam an elbow into Rossco's ribs and he yipes like a baby. "Fuck me, bruh. Why you always be hating on me? What I do to you?"

Glancing over my shoulder, I roll my eyes at the big oaf, who stands at least another five inches above me, with broad shoulders, and a chest like a brick wall. All of which make him such a great d-man.

"That's because you're always an idiot."

This elicits a snort out of the typically reserved Nils, who walks ahead as we continue down the corridor toward the exit and our private underground carpark.

Before getting to the door of his new custom Range Rover, Rossy stops and gives me a smirk.

"If I'm such an idiot, then how come I have my own foundation, eh?" Rossy straightens his shoulders, lifting one proudly in a *look at me go* gesture.

A year ago, Rossco established a charitable foundation to support youth hockey for kids in foster care, sick kids, and for the families who couldn't financially afford to shell out the expenses that come with the sport. It was something near and dear to his heart because he himself was raised in a poor household and the only way he got to play was through a Boys and Girls Club of Canada. The foundation has already raised over fifteen million, and he's contributed over a million of his own earnings, too.

Nils pipes in, "Yeah, but don't you have other people run it for you, Rossy?"

"Well, yeah. My sister does but I'm still involved, you know? That counts."

"Whatever makes you feel better about yourself, Rossy," I chirp.

"Ahh, bite me, you guys," he grumbles, opening the back door and tossing in his bag. "I'm telling Ali neither one of you are going to be the December model for our next year's charity calendar."

Nils and I exchange a look and hoot in laughter, the sound reverberating off the concrete of the underground ramp.

I snap my fingers with a theatrical swing of my arm.

"Aww, shucks, Rossy. My feelings are hurt," I say in a whiny voice, my mouth turning into a pout. "I guess you'll have to do the naked Santa pose for the December page all by yourself."

The slam of his car door is the response we get, and our laughter is drowned out by the sounds of an Ozzy song blaring from inside Rossco's car. He peels out of the spot, but then slows down, and opens his window as he inches closer.

"Better yet, I'll make you guys wear the elf costumes," he says with an evil cackle. Then he flips us off as he speeds toward the exit.

"Well shit. My wife is gonna love that." Nils says, a grin ticking up the corners of his bearded mouth.

I chortle with glee. "Guess we just became calendar elves."

Nils laughs again and gives me a hand-clasp of goodbye.

"Check ya later."

"Yeah, see ya later, Lundy."

Just as I'm about to get into my car, I hear Cale call my name.

"Yo, Ax!"

I peer over my shoulder to see him jogging toward me from the exit doors, his gym bag hanging across his torso and swinging and bouncing as he runs. I lean on the car door and wait for him to catch up.

"Hey, I didn't get a chance to ask in there"—he nods his chin toward the arena—"but would you want to come over after the Chicago game Saturday and officially meet Sommer?"

"Sommer your wife, not summer the season, right?" I laugh at my own joke, and he rolls his eyes.

"Yeah, fuckwad, my wife." Cale runs a hand through his hair. "I'm trying to introduce her to my friends, so she feels... I don't know. Like part of my life."

"Is she feeling okay? I mean, you know..."

He gives me a tight smile, his eyes not quite meeting mine. "She tells me she's doing fine and that the treatments are going okay. I know she gets tired quickly, though. Which is why I thought you and your new girl could come over for dinner and we could all just chill. No late-night barhopping or anything like that."

I give him a puzzled look. "My new girl?"

Costa looks around like he's not in on the prank or something. "Well, yeah. That girl Halle. I heard you two were dating."

"What the fuck? Where'd you hear that?"

He lifts a shoulder. "I don't know. Rumor has it you were spotted having lunch and then you were spending time at her place."

"Jesus Christ. The rumor mill around here is worse than a fucking hair salon." I run a frustrated hand through my hair and expel a breath of air. "The rumor is wrong, though. We're just friends."

He raises his hands defensively and then dismisses this without further commentary. As a friend should.

"Okay, okay. Sorry. Well, if you change your mind, feel free to bring a date, Halle or otherwise."

Cale pats me on the shoulder and dashes off toward his car, shouting at me as he goes, "After Saturday's game. See ya!"

Baffled, I start my car and head toward the arterial roads, reflecting over Cale's assumption and the rumor floating around the team already.

What if I did ask Halle to come with me? Would she be interested?

And am I so adamant about the friends label to convince my teammates of my relationship with Halle, or am I trying to convince myself?

Could Halle and I pick up where we left off? Is she as interested as I am?

My feelings and attraction for her are stronger than ever and go well beyond friendship. In the past, I chased after her and got what I wanted.

But things are vastly different now. I need to regain Halle's trust before I can win her heart.

As my mom has always told me, there's only one only way to find out.

Do it.

26

Halle

After unexpectedly taking several conse-quetive sick days off from my new job, I had to get caught up on a ton of reporting upon my return before I could pull the data I needed to prep for my presentation today, my first one at our regular staff meeting.

The meeting was supposed to be earlier in the week, but because I was out, Trevor moved it to... *today.*

Now, as I carry my laptop, notepad, and pen into the conference room just down the hall from our bank of cubicles, nerve pangs hit me in my belly. This is the first time I have to present in front of my new team.

I've really enjoyed getting to know my teammates, especially PJ. I've come to find out that PJ is brilliant and can regurgitate stats like nobody's business, but he has the maturity of a twelve-year-old boy, which can prove to be annoying. He is also hooked on watching KPop Demon Hunters and listening to the soundtrack on repeat, which is also a bit annoying. I swear, Lenni has a higher maturity level than that kid.

And then there's Anna, our team's statistician. Over the past month, her system knowledge and willingness to train me have been invaluable and because of it, we've become close personally. She asked me out to lunch again before I got sick, and she and her partner have invited Lenni and me over for a spa day at their house soon.

Sanjay is the video coach who reviews all the video clips from each game. He provides valuable insight into each player's strengths and recognizes the challenges which he then passes on to the coaches.

As I'm the first one in the room, I'm uncertain whether there's a seating order around the table, so I grab the chair nearest to the back wall, leaving my back to the wall of windows that overlook the practice rink. The room is like a fishbowl, surrounded by glass. On one side is the rink below and on the other, more windows give a view of the hallway for the offices. When the team is at home, we can easily watch them practice right below us. My brothers get super excited when I send them short video snaps of the boys practice sessions.

It's been fun to come in here with a cup of coffee and watch the team do their thing. I've been particularly interested in watching one of the best right wingers in the league—aka the Ax Man—as he works on his skating form and stickhandling.

Trevor walks into the room and does a quick head-count check around the table.

"Okay, peeps. I'm glad everyone could join us today and that our newest member is back and fully recovered." He offers me a warm smile, and I feel my face and neck heat. Trevor's tone isn't admonishing nor patronizing in any way. It's genuine and sincere. "I'm sure you've all met Halle, but just in case, let's give her a warm Vikings welcome."

Everyone raises their arms and chants, "SKOL!" three times, then pounds on the table like warriors going into battle. I cover the embarrassed smile on my face with my hand, my eyes flashing in surprise.

Once that's over, they go around the table, each introducing themselves, even though I know them all. When it comes to Anna, she gives me a knowing grin. "I'm so glad you're here, Halle."

I return the smile and immediately feel the tension depart my body. I've been so nervous about this presentation and knowing she's in my corner helps calm my nerves.

If there's one thing in this world that makes me want to hide and quake in my shoes, it's having to speak in front of people. I'm naturally an introvert by nature, and I've always been good with math and loved hockey, which is why I was so drawn to numbers and sports analytics.

Numbers and data don't expect you to make small talk or share personal information like people do.

"Halle, we firmly believe in getting to know each person on our team and treating them like family members. We use the assessments you took your first week as a way to help you reach your goals and tap into your unique strengths. If you don't mind, why don't you share your top three strengths with the team, as well as a little bit about your background and how you ended up with the Vikings organization?"

Thankfully, I don't have to stand up, which is helpful for my shaking legs. I clasp my sweaty palms together on my lap and smile like I'm not petrified to have all eyes on me.

It's exactly why the top strengths identified through this assessment are what they are because I'm a numbers geek.

During my first week on the job, the HR rep had me complete a very lengthy skills assessment and afterward, we sat down and reviewed the results, identifying my key traits and areas of opportunity within the organization. None of them came as a shock, but it was interesting to learn how I can use them in the workplace to be a better team player and grow my career.

It makes me curious to know whether Dane and his teammates took the same test.

"Thanks, Trevor. Well, it should come as no surprise based on my job here, but my top three strengths are Analytical, Responsibility, and Achiever." Everyone chuckled. I had a feeling there were more of us here than I originally thought. "I've always been good with math and science, so when I was looking at universities, I already knew I'd major in a STEM program." I clear my throat and glance away at the glass window. "My college path wasn't as straight as I'd hoped, though. As most of you know, I became a mother to my daughter Lennon at a very young age, so I switched to an online program that allowed me to finish my degree from my home in Calgary." I inhale a large intake of breath and try not to worry about what everyone thinks of me as I exhale.

Although I've gotten to know some of this crew in the past month, it's hard to judge what they might think about unwed single mothers. Honestly, it took me a long time to come to terms with the fact that some people are just opinionated assholes and I don't have to validate their viewpoints.

It's not my problem, it's theirs.

Trevor suddenly jumps in with his own comments, giving me a chance to catch my breath.

"Your commitment to finishing your degree after such a challenge demonstrates your drive to succeed. Well done, Halle."

I chew on the inside of my cheek, flustered by his encouragement and support. It's like having my dad here to root me on.

"Thank you, but I didn't do it all alone. I had family around to help me."

My team members nod their support, and I see quite a few encouraging smiles.

"That's exactly what I'm talking about. We're not just part of a team here, we're a family of sorts, too." Trevor sweeps an arm over the table, gesturing to everyone seated around it. "Just like the players out on the ice, we don't win without each other. It's never a one-person solo job. There is no I in Team."

Anna locks eyes with me and jumps in with her question. "Can you tell us why you choose to move to Vancouver to work for a *hockey* team, since your family is all back in Calgary?"

Now this is a question I have an answer for.

I snap on a delighted smile and tilt my head confidently.

"I love hockey. I grew up in a hockey-loving home where my dad and two brothers both played. In high school, I also worked for the juniors organization in our hometown. It's just part of my DNA."

And then under someone's breath, I hear them mutter, "And her daughter's."

I'm stunned by the whispered remark and I see Anna shoot a look down the table to where a few other people from other departments sit. Was it said with intentional malice? Did someone come to that conclusion because they saw Dane with Lenni?

Regardless, I now know I'm going to need to figure out how to navigate that minefield without it blowing up in my face.

Secrets have a way of coming out. And when and if mine does, I fear the discovery of the deceit will leave me vulnerable and accountable for my actions.

27

D^{ane}

The team is on a three-game winning streak, and it feels fucking great.

Tonight, we played against Pittsburgh on their home turf and whomped them five to two. The first goal was made by me with an assist by the rookie center Lyons, who we've nicknamed Simba, our team's lion cub.

Lyons fought for the puck against a Pittsburgh defender and kicked it out to where I was at the top of the crease. I put my stick down and drove toward the post, flipping the puck right over the shoulder of the goalie. There was nothing he could do as the puck deflected up into the upper right part of the net.

My season is off to a fan-fucking-tastic start, and my stats are fire. There's a part of me that revels in the knowledge that Halle is seeing these stats in her reports, and I wonder if she thinks of me when my name pops up in her data.

Now that we're on the long team flight back to Vancouver, I pull out my phone and start a text. It's a three-hour time difference, so by my estimation, Lenni should have gone to bed by now, hopefully leaving some time for Halle to relax.

> Me: Hey Cherry. Did you watch the game tonight?

I see the dots and get a secret thrill. Our exchanges haven't been much since she's recovered and hasn't required my help, and I've tried to give her space. But each time we chat, it reminds me of our eighteen-year-old selves. When we were apart, we texted constantly. It was always fun and flirty and left me hard as a rock for her.

Not much has changed there.

> Cherry: What game? Don't know what you're talking about.

I laugh and Costa, who is next to me and reading a book, cuts me a look. I mouth *sorry* and return to my phone.

> Me: Oh, we're playing it that way, are we?

Me: You know. The greatest game in the world. The greatest team. And the

greatest player.

Cherry: OMG! I didn't realize Gretzky played tonight. Wow. That's so cool. He's such a legend.

Me: Very funny, Cherry. Don't hurt yourself by cracking yourself up.

Cherry: Nothing funny about the GOAT.

Me: Yeah, yeah, yeah. He's the GOAT. I get it. But come on, Cherry. Admit it. You know good, eh?

I recline back in my seat and stretch out my legs, crossing my feet at the ankles. It's never comfortable wearing dress shoes on the plane, so I've slipped them off and am only in my socks, wiggling my unrestricted toes.

Cherry: You don't need me to stroke your ego, hockey boy.

Actually, I do. I care deeply about what Halle thinks about me. Whether she is excited when I score a goal or make an assist, I want to know she's watching me in action. Her approval of me matters.

> Me: You have no idea how hard I'm trying to restrain myself from making an inappropriate and dirty response. You teed it up for a good one.

There's a pause. I see the dots flash and then disappear. Then again. And again. I may have made a mistake directing the conversation into something sexual.

Fuck. I crossed a line I shouldn't have. My body deflates and I slam my eyes shut, pressing my head against the airline seat. Then I feel my phone vibrate in my hand, and my entire body vibrates with urgency to read her reply.

> Cherry: Oh, you mean, stroke your dick?
>
> Cherry: In your dreams, hockey boy.

Oh shit, she went there. I smile so broadly that when Canners walks by from his trip to the bathroom, he levels me a strange look.

I read the texts again. That's my girl. Sweet, sexy and sassy.

And yeah, I know she's not mine. But the more I deny it, the more it feels like a lie trapped on my tongue. I've tried to be mature about this and do the right thing by keeping my distance, but the more I do, the less satisfied I feel.

There's something missing in my life when Halle isn't in it.

Me: You said it, not me. I think it's your dream, Cherry.

Cherry: Ha! Only those crazy fever dreams I had when I was sick.

Me: So, you admit you've been dreaming about me. I knew it.

Cherry: I think those are called nightmares.

Me: Hmm… as long you're dreaming about me… you can call it what you want.

Her keystrokes stop, and I know I should redirect this conversation before things get too far off the friendship course. Plus, I want to ask her out on a date, so I need to step back and take it slow.

Me: How's it going now that you're back at work?

Cherry: Much better. Thanks. I like my boss a lot. I've made a friend in Anna, but I feel like I don't fit in with the rest of my department. They see me as an outsider still.

Me: What do you mean?

Cherry: IDK. I'm just not at the same point in life as they are. You know… I have Lenni.

Cherry: I just get a judgey vibe from a few of them.

Me: Shit. What's up with the haters? You're one of the nicest people I know.

Cherry: That's sweet. Thank you. Maybe I'm just overly sensitive.

Me: Want me to slash them with my stick?

Cherry: No fighting, Dane. I don't want to see you in the penalty box again.

Cherry: Like tonight.

Me: I knew it! You did watch the game.

Cherry: Fiiiiine. Lenni and I watched until she fell asleep. It only proves that your hockey skills bored her to sleep.

Me: It proves to me that you like watching me play.

Cherry: Good night, Dane.

Me: Wait, wait, wait! I have something to ask you.

Cherry: What?

Me: Cale Costa's wife, Sommer, will be in town this weekend. He invited me over to hang with them, and he asked me to bring someone.

Me: Would you come with me? It'll be after the afternoon game on Saturday but not too late.

Cherry: Um, no. In case you've forgotten,
I have Lenni. Duh.

Me: Let me take care of that. I really want
to spend time with you.

Cherry: Maybe. I'll have to think about it.

Me: Okay. I'll check back on Friday.

Cherry: Sure. Okay. Good night, Dane.
For real this time.

Me: Night, Cherry Bomb. And you can
feel free to dream about me.

That's the last thing I get from her, and my screen goes dark. I slip my phone back in the pocket of my pants and lean back again, settling in and allowing my heavy head to rest against the neck pillow.

There's so many feelings tied up when it comes to Halle that it's hard to separate the girl I once knew from the woman I know now. She's still funny and quick-witted, but her edges aren't as sharp as they once were. Halle is still the confident woman she always was, but she's softened with motherhood. And that is sexy as fuck.

It only makes me admire her more, makes me want to be someone she can rely on to help her and Lenni, but it's more than that. I care for Halle in a way I've never cared for another woman.

And then there's this pull of attraction I can't deny. All it took was seeing her again and a fire that had long been

28

H alle

"Why the hell wouldn't you say yes? There's nothing to think about. Just fucking go."

I stare into the video screen, where Carmy is currently giving me hell over my indecisive answer to Dane's request.

I sigh. "Carm, it's not that simple. And keep your swearing voice down. Lenni might overhear."

"It is that simple," she spits out in a shushed whisper. "You're just making it extra difficult."

Sometimes, Carm just doesn't get my reality or see things from my perspective. She's not a working woman raising a child on her own. Carmy doesn't have to worry about taking care of anyone but herself.

While she's my best friend and I love her to death, her outlook on life is skewed and has been since we first met.

She was born into wealth and privilege, an only child doted on by her parents and spoiled to the point of annoyance. Carm doesn't have to worry about anything but passing her boards.

"I can't go out with Dane Axelrod. Period. End of story."

Carm sits up against her headboard and scowls at me. "You're so stubborn, Hal. Goddammit. You drive me nuts sometimes."

"Right back atcha, bitch," I counter, comically scrunching my face at her. She bursts out laughing and I follow suit.

Then her expression turns serious. And a serious Carmen is deadly. It's why I know she will be a great prosecutor someday. I'd hate to be on the other side of a courtroom from her.

"Listen. You have an opportunity to reconnect with the father of your child. Even if it doesn't go anywhere, it still gives you the chance to form a new relationship with him. In the end, Lenni can see her parents together in a respectful and friendly arrangement."

"You're saying I should go on a date with Dane for Lenni's sake?"

She chuckles. "No, bitch. I'm saying, go out with Dane, get down and dirty and your clocks wound, then decide how you want to play it. Either way, you get some dick. And we both know that's what you need."

"My clocks wound?" I repeat, smacking my palm

across my forehead. "Does everything always have to be about sex with you?"

Carmy leans into the screen so that her eyes and nose zoom in close. "Girl, need I remind you? Sex is what got you into this situation in the first place. Maybe it can help get you out of it."

"I don't need to get out of anything!" I grouse like the cranky, sex-starved woman my friend says I am. But I lie and try to make myself believe it too. "I'm just fine the way things are. I'm happy. Lenni's happy."

"Sure, sure. Everyone is just fine. Except that Lenni is going to someday—probably sooner rather than later—ask more about her father. If you don't do it now, there could come a shitload of resentment in the future."

I growl because Carmen's right. Lenni's already expressed interest in who her dad is and why she doesn't have one. So far, I've been able to easily divert the conversation and downplay the question by telling her that she has everyone she needs in her life.

But am I being fair by keeping this tightly held secret?

Am I gambling with her future? And hurting mine in the process?

I know Dane has been patiently waiting for me to let us tell Lenni. He wants the three of us to sit down and explain to her that Dane is her daddy. But even that opens the floodgates to a myriad of questions I'm not sure how to answer.

Ones like: Where has Dane been? Why don't we all live together? Did Dane not love her?

How do I answer any of those complex questions in a way that a four-year-old can understand?

It all boils down to one thing: I'm scared to reveal the truth.

The reason my daughter hasn't known her father is because I kept them both in the dark. And now that he's in our lives, the deceit becomes harder to live with.

As I begin to re-examine the decision I've stuck to all these years, the memories start to dismantle themselves piece by piece, and the picture zooms into focus clearer than ever before.

I've been protecting my own heart, not just my daughter's.

Carmen flaps her hand in front of the camera, drawing my attention back to our conversation. "Hello. Are you still with me, Hal?"

I blink away my remorse. My voice cracks over words that come out in a ragged whisper. "Yeah, okay. You're right."

Her eyes grow comically wide. "What? Can you repeat that? Did you just admit that I'm right?"

She whoops out a loud, gleeful noise and throws her head back with a cackle, pointing her index fingers alternately to the ceiling in a dance of celebration. "I'm right. I'm right. I'm so fucking riiiiiight."

"Oh, for fuck's sake. I'm hanging up on you now, you brat," I warn, sticking my tongue out like a juvenile. "You're being a dick."

"Fine, sorry. I got carried away, but can you blame

me? Usually, you're the voice of reason. It's just so out of character for you to be wrong."

I flip her off. "I'm not wrong, per se. You just happen to have a strong argument and case. You are a lawyer, after all."

"Lawyer-to-be. If I ever get through these exams with my head intact." She scrubs a hand over her face. "Jesus, it's killing me. But your boy troubles are a good distraction. Thanks for that."

"So glad my chaotic life can be such a helpful distraction for you." I snort just as a text pops up on my screen. "Hold on a second. I have an incoming text. It could be my dad."

I tap the phone and the video of Carmy's face disappears as I click over to the text app. When I see who it's from, my stomach does a somersault.

> Hockey Boy: I'm here to officially invite you out on a date.

Here? Here, where?

The next text follows closely behind, and I jump off the couch in a panic.

> Hockey Boy: Come to the door. I'm on your front porch.

I spin around in a circle and can hear Carmy on the line saying, "What's going on, Hal?" at the same time there's a knock on the door.

"Carmy, holy shit." I click back to the video chat, and

my eyes are wild with panic. "Dane's here. Right now. At my house."

"Well then, go answer the freaking door, Halle," she instructs me matter-of-factly. And then in a hushed whisper, she says, "And I hope you've shaved your legs and pussy in the last year."

I don't have time for a snotty response before the line goes black and she disappears from my screen, leaving me standing in the middle of the room, about to let in trouble.

I do a quick scan of my attire, completely spacing on what I threw on earlier when we got home from work. My cropped Vikings T-shirt has a stain on it from the SpaghettiOs I made for Lenni's dinner, and my bottom half is clad in only a pair of cotton pajama shorts. No socks or shoes, and my hair is hanging sideways in a messy ponytail.

Carm's comment about my shaving needs has me doing a quick fly-by of my shins, rubbing the bottom of my foot over my calf to verify the state of my stubble. All good there.

I unlock the deadbolts and swing the door open. If I'm dressed in comfy wear, Dane is blindingly handsome in a gray suit jacket and crisp white shirt, the top two buttons undone to show a bit of his chest hair. I swallow thickly, my tummy doing a shimmy of desire over his appearance.

Dane's eyes cast a slow, sensual gaze over my body, his perusal sending pinpricks of pleasure as he hovers at my bare stomach and my breasts before he stops at my mouth.

I can't help but bite down on my bottom lip.

"What are you doing here?" I ask, glancing at the time on the phone I'm still clutching in my hand. "It's late and I have a sleeping child in here."

He leans casually against the doorjamb and from behind his back pulls out a bouquet of pink Gerber daisies surrounded by an assortment of greenery and white baby's breath.

I reach to grab the flowers from his grasp, but he doesn't let go.

Instead, he holds my gaze as he steps forward across the threshold, and a slow smile unfurls across his handsome face.

"Halle, will you go out on a date with me?"

How the hell do I say no to that?

29

———

Dane

"Come on, Cherry. What do you say?" I ask boldly, hiding the nerves I felt all the way here from the airport. "You deserve a night out for yourself."

Halle plucks the flowers from my hand with a gruff tug and walks toward the kitchen, where she opens and closes cabinets. I manage to keep my eyes off her perfect ass as she bends over to pull out a glass vase from a lower cupboard. But just barely—the temptation is strong.

"Dane ..." she says in that argumentative tone of hers, drawing out the syllables slowly. It dawns on me that she might say no.

I'm not sure if I've ever been turned down before. A jittery feeling unfolds in my chest. It's the same swell of emotion that resided there when we played in the first round of the playoffs and were on the cusp of a loss.

When she swings back around, vase in her hand, I'm right there, grabbing the heavy piece out of her grip and setting it down on the counter behind her. Halle's lips press tight as she grips the edge of the counter and I lean in, positioning my hands next to hers.

She sucks in a deep breath and I smirk, knowing that I'm getting to her. I duck my chin to meet her gaze. Her eyes blaze hot and bold, but hold an uncertainty, too. A nervousness.

"Do I make you nervous being this close to you, Cherry?"

"No," she snaps, the flash in her eyes sparking with defiant intensity. There it is. There's the girl I remember. "Why would it?"

I snicker, closing in further until I'm a breath away from her face. I inhale her sweet citrus and honey scent and tuck a loose lock of her hair behind her ear. I want to lean in and suck her earlobe between my teeth. I close my eyes and grip the countertop, digging my fingers to gain control.

"Because I think you want me to kiss you. To lean in and take your lips, kiss you so fucking hard you feel it in your toes." My voice is husky and thick. My body hums with the electricity that sizzles in blistering sparks between us.

Halle presses a shaky hand flat against my chest and pushes. I concede and take a step back, but we still remain toe-to-toe.

"I'm not looking to be kissed, by you or anyone else."

She sidesteps past me and picks up the vase, depositing it on the small kitchen table. "And if you remember, I can't go anywhere with you because I have a daughter at home to take care of."

I lean my hip against the sink and shake my head. "I haven't forgotten about Lenni. Which is why I've already lined up a babysitter."

Halle's head snaps back around so fast she could be in contention for a role in the next Exorcist movie. Her voice rises a few octaves. "You did *what*?"

She stalks toward me, and I can almost see smoke and sparks spewing from her body. It gives new meaning to the term smokeshow.

I cock my head, keeping my gaze leveled on her, a grin affixed to my mouth. I love it when she gets ruffled and flustered like this. Exactly how it was the first time I met her when she had cherry slushie spilled all over herself. It was the cutest and sexiest thing I've ever seen.

I repeat myself and lift a shoulder. "I. Got. A. Babysitter. For Lenni."

"You... why... who... gah! You are so infuriatingly presumptuous." She raises her hands in balled-up fists, shaking them in the air between us.

I place both palms over her fists and guide them down, wrapping my fingers around her wrists to gently hold them between us.

"I'm trying to help," I counter, letting go of her hands so they drop to her sides. "Since Nils and Helena's nanny will be watching their kids while they're at Cale's with us, and I hear Lenni and Elise are besties now, it's an easy win-win for Lenni to join them."

This still doesn't get the reaction I'd hoped for because Halle is still pretty mad. Her cheeks are flushed red, her lips pursed tightly, and there are two angry little grooves that have formed between her brows.

I can't help myself. I reach out and smooth the lines down the bridge of her nose. She swats my hand away, and I chuckle.

"Ooh... I really like this side of you. Angry little tiger." I curl my hand into a claw-like gesture.

She makes a face, and I reach for her wrist again.

"Come with me so we can sit down and talk." I nod toward the other room, then let go of her hand and wait for her response.

"Fine. But I have a lot to say."

"I'm sure you do."

I gesture for her to proceed and when we get to the couch, and she plops down on the cushion. I take the spot next to her.

"Halle, stop being so stubborn."

Definitely the wrong thing to say. Her head spins so fast it feels like something out of *The Exorcist*, and she glares at me haughtily.

I throw up my hands in defeat. "Sorry. I didn't mean it that way. Okay, I should've consulted you first..."

She touches the tip of her nose with a finger. "Bingo!" she interjects, tossing me a fiery look. God, what I wouldn't give to see the heat in those eyes while she was naked and on top of me.

But I digress.

I tentatively place my palm on top of her knee and we both stare at it. Her skin is warm and soft. My fingers itch to caress the silk canvas of her leg.

I see a flicker of something flash in the pools of her teal eyes.

"I arranged it all beforehand because I knew you'd use it as an excuse not to go out with me. But it wasn't on a whim. Give me a little credit, here, Hal." I give her my boyishly charming smile and bat my eyelashes, going in for the kill shot. "You already know Helena and trust that her nanny has been vetted. And Lenni will have fun playing with her new friend, Elise."

And there it is. I see the moment she relents. Her entire body sags, the tension loosens from her stiff shoulders, and her facial muscles relax.

She avoids my gaze, so I lean over and look her in the eyes.

They are a shimmering sea of blue-green ocean.

"Well? Do you forgive me for being so—what did you call me? Infuriatingly presumptuous?"

Halle rolls her eyes and fights a smile that quirks up on the corners of her mouth.

Finally, she speaks. "I'm still mad at you. But I can forgive you, even though I think you only did it for your own benefit."

I snort loudly and crash back into the sofa cushions.

She shushes me, and I remember that Lenni is asleep down the hall. I still have a lot to learn.

"Oh please," I whisper. "We both know you get the biggest benefit of all." With my head pressed against the top of the couch, I slowly turn it toward Halle, offering her a cheesy grin. "You get to hang with me."

"Gah! You are so full of yourself." She smacks a palm over my chest, and I snag her wrist in my grasp. Then I raise her hand to my lips and kiss the top of her knuckles.

"But you love that about me." I kiss her hand again and then turn to place a kiss at the top of her head before I stand up and walk myself to the front door.

When I turn around, I think I see something in Halle's eyes I haven't seen in a long time.

Longing.

And it gives me hope.

"Good night, Cherry. See you tomorrow."

30

———

Halle

After running our Saturday morning errands to buy groceries for the week and do several loads of laundry—because there is always laundry—Lennon and I spend some time down at the neighborhood park. They have a newly updated kids' play area, and my daughter literally turns into a monkey, climbing and sliding down all the chutes and ladders.

When we get back to the house, there's a manila envelope with my name on it propped up against the front door.

"What's that, Mama?" Lenni asks as she hands it to me, just as curious as I am to find out what's inside.

I unlock the front door and look around to see if a delivery truck is in the neighborhood. "I'm not sure. I don't remember ordering anything."

Lenni sprints inside the minute the door swings open,

running toward the kitchen to wait for the midmorning snack I promised her in the car. I follow behind and deposit the bags of groceries onto the counter, eyeing the envelope in my hand.

It's light and has the Vancouver Vikings logo at the top. Odd, because I'm not expecting anything from work. I suppose it could be some leftover new employee benefit information, but the contents don't weigh much.

I set Lenni up at the table and get her some Goldfish crackers and the sliced apples from the fridge, and she digs in ravenously, as if she's never tasted food before. I chuckle at the similarities between her and Dane in that department. Then, unable to contain my burning curiosity any longer, I tear it open and extract a folded note.

Inside, a ticket and a VIP pass are attached together inside with a paperclip.

The note reads:

Dear Halle,

Game is at 1 p.m. I have arranged for a driver to pick you and Lenni up at noon. (Don't worry, the car is equipped with a newly installed kids car seat.) She will be dropped off at the Lundrens' house, where the nanny will take good care of the girls. You and Helena will then be routed to Cale's house to pick up his wife, Sommer, and you'll all sit in the Vikings' friends and family seats. You'll receive passes for down-stairs and the family lounge—Helena knows how it works, so don't worry—where we'll join you post-game.

 I'm looking forward to seeing you tonight.
Root for #25 tonight.
Dane

Butterflies flitter in my belly and then turn to anxious flutters when I check the time on my phone. Son of a biscuit! It's already eleven a.m. and I need to shower and get myself ready, as well as get together a bag for Lenni to bring.

Then I'm struck with a thought. Will we need overnight bags? Is there a sleepover planned?

Will I be staying the night with Dane?

Nerves ricochet through my bloodstream over the chance—although slim—that I might sleep with Dane. It's been a long time. He's literally my first and my last since having Lenni.

"Hey, sweet pea?"

"Yeah, Mama?" she says through a nibble of a cracker.

"We need to hurry up and get ready to go because we're going to have a fun adventure this afternoon."

Her face lights up with a bright toothy grin. "Weally? Where are we going? Disneyland?"

I can't contain the laughter that bubbles up from my

throat. My sweet little girl is in love with all things Disney princess and since learning about the happiest place on Earth, it's all she ever wants to do and talk about. The Sleeping Beauty Castle is number one on her list.

"Not Disneyland today, baby. But remember your new friend Elise?"

"Uh-huh."

I get a washcloth from the drawer, wet it in the sink, and do a quick cleanup of Lenni's face and hands.

"Well, you get to play at her house today. Won't that be fun?"

Suddenly, her features grow serious with a scrunch of her face. "Will you be there, Mama?"

Although she's come out of her shell considerably since starting at the Vikings daycare, there have been a few times during her drop-offs where she's gotten very emotional and clingy.

I suppose it's natural and just a stage she's going through, but it makes my heart hurt so much to have to let go of my baby. It's the perils of parenthood.

I stroke a hand over her shiny—albeit tangly—blond hair and offer an encouraging smile.

"No, honey. I'm going with the grown-ups to the hockey game."

To my surprise, Lenni leaps from the chair with a whoop of excitement. Then she spreads her legs in a jumping-jack motion and raises her hand in the air, making a chopping motion that resembles splitting wood. I stare at my daughter in disbelief.

"Let's go, Ax!" She dances around and continues to chant and chop. "SKOL, SKOL, SKOL!"

I'm momentarily stunned at this display of Vikings pride.

"Where did you learn this?" I mimic the gesture, and she grins, another characteristic strikingly similar to her father.

"From Ax," she states proudly, then runs off toward her bedroom, leaving me standing in my kitchen and realizing I've just lost all control over this situation.

Her father has already influenced his daughter and endeared himself to her.

I stare down at the note again. And to me, too.

THE GAME IS A NAIL-BITER, ending in a tie in regulation and going into OT. As the crowd thins for bathroom breaks and concession-stand runs during the fifteen-minute intermission, Helena and I explain to Sommer—who came clean about not being a hockey aficionado—about the rules of OT.

"Because they've tied, they'll go into a five-minute overtime period, and the first team to score wins," Helena says, taking a sip of the beer she's nursed for the better part of the last period. She'd mentioned earlier that she's become a lightweight after she finished nursing Ingrid a few months ago.

I can totally relate, although I never was much interested in drinking beer in the first place. If I have a choice, I'll go for a cocktail or two, but wine and beer don't really do it for me.

But who needs booze when this night has been a blast. The three of us have clicked in a way I've never had with women outside of Carmen. We all come from different backgrounds and are in different places in our lives, but both Helena and Sommer are solid, genuine people. They are down to earth, friendly, and not focused on fame or being social media influencers.

In fact, I took a selfie with both women earlier, and Helena requested that I not post it on any social media. I hadn't been planning on it but asked her why.

Her eyes grew sad and downcast. "It's hard to be the wife of someone who has a lot of fans."

She left it at that, and I made a point not to press any further. But I'll ask her for the story later if she's comfortable sharing.

Sommer, also, is easy to talk to. I was taken aback when she told me the incredible way she and Cale met and got married on the same night. As the saying goes, when you know you know.

I wish I were that sure about anything in my life and could decide that quickly. I'm always riddled with indecision and uncertainty about what I should or shouldn't do.

Case in point: Dane.

Sommer's follow-up question draws me back to the conversation.

"So, what happens if neither team scores during overtime?"

"They have a shootout!" I exclaim, then lean in with a wide grin. "And Cale had the best record in the league last season for shootout goals."

Sommer's face brightens with the heat of a blush, and she chews on her lip. "Oh."

Helena gives her a friendly bump on the shoulder with hers. "How does it feel to be married to the captain and highest scorer on the team?"

"Strange. Weird. Unreal." She turns her eyes down to her lap, where her hands are clasped in a tight grasp. "Obviously, I'm not a hockey fan, so this is all new. I didn't know Cale was a hockey player when we met. He's just a nice guy."

"Nice? That's what attracted you to him?" Helena prods, eyes flashing with teasing mischief. "Come on... not his eyes, or his chiseled features... or that flow?"

Sommer giggles, shaking her head. "Flow?"

Helena and I exchange a look and laugh. I pat Sommer's knee. "You have a lot to learn about hockey, my friend."

The way she describes Cale's compassionate nature has me thinking of Dane and how he's not only interested in me, but is stepping up for Lennon. I guess you could say he has stake in the game and is doing it for the right reasons.

As if reading my thoughts, Sommer quirks a knitted brow.

"You haven't mentioned much about you and Dane. There's something going on between you two," she observes. "Are you going to spill the tea with us?"

I've tried keeping my interest in Dane's game tonight low-key and under wraps, cheering loudly for the entire team, not just Ax's performance. But I'm not known for my poker face. I'm sure my interest in him is displayed like a billboard sign in Times Square.

"Honestly, I don't know what's going on. We have history, but it was short-lived. I guess we're just exploring what it looks like now."

"If you want my opinion," Helena adds, a smile pulling at the corners of her lips. "I think it looks really good on you both. I've never seen Dane so smitten. And it's no secret he has a reputation for being..."

"A player?" I interrupt on a laugh.

"Yeah, but not in a bad way. There's just a lot of turnover, and he's not into serious relationships. But you" —Helena pats my thigh with her gloved hand—"are a good fit for him. You're responsible, stable, smart, and so damn cute."

"Thanks," I say, blushing at her compliment. Sitting with these two women gives me the courage to share a little more. "I do like Dane... a lot. But I have more than myself to think about."

They both share sympathetic looks and let the conversation drop. Soon, the refs return to the ice, and the teams skate out of their respective tunnels.

"Ooh, look," Sommer exclaims, pointing to the ice.

"They're ready to play again. This is so exciting. Let's go, Vikings!"

Our attention returns to the center of the arena, and we chant and cheer together for our team, the men we're rooting for looking like the Vikings they are as they head into overtime play.

31

———

ane
Nothing compares to winning a hard-fought game and then following it up with a great night out with friends. And tonight was that kind of night.

Cale and Sommer had catered a dinner at their house, and we spent the evening playing stupid card games and getting to know the women, especially Sommer. Every time I managed to look at Halle, her face was glowing. It's given me a full heart to know I was able to offer her this adult night out.

She may not ever admit it to me, but after all the stress of moving, starting a new job, getting Lenni settled in a new daycare arrangement, and recovering from her illness, she undoubtedly needed a night to enjoy adult company.

So did I. And hanging out with the two other couples has been good, clean fun, but not dull.

And as we near the end of the night, I don't want to let Halle go.

We haven't had a chance to talk about the things between us or what's ahead. It's the elephant that sits in the room between us, and I want to kick it out and close that distance.

"Thanks for teaching our daughter the Ax move, by the way," she jokes from the passenger seat of my car, sarcasm dripping from her tone as she demonstrates the motion for me. "Lenni wouldn't stop doing it when I told her about today's plans."

I laugh, briefly taking my eyes off the road to smile at her. It's surreal to have her alone in my car again. We spent a shitload of time together in the front and back-seat of my old Jeep, talking, joking, and making out. And when things got really intense, she'd climb on top of me with my seat laid out flat, and we'd fog up the windows from the heat of our bodies.

We were desperate and wild for each other, and I never wanted anyone as much as I wanted Halle. I was mesmerized by her smile. Her taste. Her fearlessness. And her effervescent light that outshone even the sun.

The sad part was we both knew the clock was ticking, that things would get complicated when she left for school. I may have been an adolescent on the cusp of adulthood, but in my heart, I was willing to go the distance. At least, I had told myself that. Halle had been right, though. We were too young, and it wouldn't have ended on a good note. I was not up to the task at the time.

But I'm ready for it now.

Knowing what I do now, I realize my desire for Halle wasn't just because I was young and horny. It was a deep gnawing centered straight in the middle of my gut. I craved her like a starving man craves food.

And that hasn't changed one bit. It's only intensified since she's returned to my life.

I grin at the fact that she didn't say *my* daughter this time. It could be just a slip of the tongue, but I want to believe she's finally turned the corner and made the decision to allow me to be part of Lenni's life.

Not as a trusted adult friend, but as her father.

That one word fills me with hope that we can move forward. Together. As a couple and as a family.

The evening is cool, but we have the windows cracked, letting the autumn night air filter in. I turn down my street, lined with maples that have all but lost their leaves, and pull into my driveway. I watch her from the corner of my eye as she scans the house in front of us.

"Is this your place?"

I turn off the ignition and shift in my seat toward her. My gaze roams over her as I drink her in.

From her unique teal-blue eyes twinkling in the light that shines through the window to the long, loose waves of her auburn hair that give even the most colorful autumn leaves a run for their money.

When I walked into the lounge after the game and

saw her wearing a red sweater that fits her like a glove, accentuating her narrow waist and incredible curves, I nearly swallowed my tongue and lost my ability to speak.

My fingers twitched to undo each cream-colored pearl button cascading down that sweater's front one by freaking one, making her body come alive as I cup each swell in the palm of my hand.

Although I gave her a hard time over not wearing any Vikings apparel to the game, her choice in clothing is still casual yet alluring. So very Cherry.

Our eyes lock and time rewinds so I'm back to where it all started. I reach for her hand and draw it to my chest, where I clutch it against me.

"I thought maybe you might want to... I don't know... see my place." It comes out more as a question than a statement.

Jesus Christ. This woman has me practically stammering over my words. Who am I right now? I'm the Ax Man—proven ladies' man, playboy, whatever you want to call me, but I don't get tongue-tied around women.

Except around Halle. She steals my breath and takes all my logic. It's like getting pummeled into the boards by a top defenseman.

When she remains silent, I continue. "No pressure, honest. I just want to spend time with yo—"

My words are stolen when Halle's lips crash over mine, and I'm stunned. I don't know which way's up or down.

She leans over the console, winds her hands behind

my neck, and kisses me with those warm, wet lips that taste better than I ever remembered. My brain finally kicks in, and I lift my hands to frame her face, sealing my mouth over hers and keeping her locked tight to me.

A hungry, feral groan rises from my chest, one that's met with a soft purr from her. My tongue strokes the seams between her lips, and she parts them to allow me access. One sweep of my tongue and I'm a goner. Every cell in my body awakens and vibrates with need.

I hesitantly pull back. With hooded eyes, I take her in, searching her expression for any signs of potential regret. Her lips are wet and swollen, her cheeks flushed. Her nipples pucker through the sweater and her chest rises and falls with a quickened breath. Then she lets out a shuttering sigh.

I lick my lips. "If you're okay with it, I'd like to take this inside. We've had enough time in cars together, don't you think?"

She chuckles and gives me a nod. "I'm more than okay."

I practically jump out of the car, sprinting to open the passenger door and offer her my hand. Halle's giggle is light and airy.

"So chivalrous," she teases, and I can't wait to touch her again.

I rake my fingers through her wavy hair and shove her back against the car door. My dick reacts instantly as I press my hips into hers, and there is no mistaking that I want her.

Halle opens her mouth to welcome my frantic need, and I swallow her gasp with my mouth. The kiss is all-consuming, an uncontained fire that ignites upon contact and threatens to overtake us with its sheer ferocity.

Her hands slide behind me and find purchase on my ass. She is so soft and willing, and I am hard and greedy.

I keep one hand tangled in her hair and glide the other to her jaw, tilting her head so I can slide my lips along the expanse of her neck.

"Fuck, you taste so sweet, Cherry. Just like you always did," I murmur against her skin, then suck along the sensitive curve, smiling when I feel her tremble in my embrace.

I grind against her. Knowing I shouldn't. Knowing we're exposed to the prying eyes of the neighbors who would just love to sell the story about Viking player Ax Axelrod and one of his many conquests.

I pull away but keep my gaze firmly set on her as I flick the buttons of her sweater. "This sweater looks so wholesome," I say, voice thick with desire. "But I want to do very unwholesome things to you."

Spinning her around, I glide my palm over her ass. "And I can't do any of those things out here. Now scoot."

Then I swat her on the butt with a wink.

32

Halle

The minute we're inside, I excuse myself to the bathroom. Mostly to give myself a much-needed pep talk and time to calm my nerves.

Dane escorts me to a powder room painted the color of the sky. I was so focused on giving myself some space from the intensity of those kisses that I didn't even look around at the interior of his home as we moved down the hallway.

In some respects, Dane is still somewhat of a stranger to me. Except for the facts he's shared and what I've googled, I know only the basics of his life since we parted. And most of the online information was stats or rumors about his love life. I avoided those tidbits.

"I'll be right over there," Dane says pointing down the hallway, his voice filled with the huskiness of desire. He stares at me long and hard, as if searching for an answer to the unspoken question of, *are you all right?*

"Thanks. I'll be right out."

He reaches to grab the door handle at the same time that I do, and our fingers touch. Electricity shoots up my arm. The corners of his mouth quirk upward. "Take your time."

Time. What a funny concept.

I've had plenty of it—five years, in fact—never expecting I'd have another moment like this with Dane. Which is why I'm so damn nervous.

The sound of the door clicking shut and the quiet that surrounds me sends me in a chaotic tailspin.

I stare at myself in the mirror and don't even recognize the woman in the reflection. I am deliciously disheveled with swollen lips and wait... what's this? I lean in to get a good look in the mirror and tug the collar of my sweater away from my neck. Right there below my ear is a red mark left from when Dane nipped and sucked the skin.

In fact, my panties are still damp from the sensation that rippled through me while he did it.

Even after all these years, Dane can get me hot and wet within seconds, all without even using his fingers or dick. What does that say about me?

I'm still as inexperienced as the virgin I was when we first met.

And he's been with loads and loads of women since then.

I wash and dry my hands as I mentally prepare myself for what comes next. I've got this. It's just like riding a bicycle. Right?

When I open the door, the sound of soft music wafts in from the main living area. I follow it down the hallway and find Dane sitting on a large L-shaped couch. His legs are propped up on a leather ottoman, one arm draped along the back of the sofa, and his soft eyes track me as I walk toward him.

He drops his hand and pats the cushion next to him. "Come here."

I swallow, and my feet don't want to move. "Dane... you need to know something... I don't think I can do this if you just want casual."

He swings his feet to the floor and pushes up to stand, then walks purposefully toward me, his eyes turning a dark steel gray as he gets closer. I'm trapped in the spotlight of his gaze, marveling at how it changes in intensity and color based on his mood.

Taking my hands in his, he lifts them both to his lips and presses a light kiss on each. The soft bristles of his beard scrape over my skin, and the sensation zaps between my thighs.

Which, I realize, is where I want his hands. So much that I ache with the need.

My breath stutters unevenly with nerves and excitement over where this is leading. What he has planned for me.

"Cherry, this is anything but casual for me. It never

has been with you. Ever." He drops our hands down to our sides and moves in another step closer so there's scarcely a breath between us. Then he begins to move side to side, swaying like a tree in the wind. Our feet move to the slow rhythm of the music in the background. "I don't deserve this second chance with you, but I don't want to lose it. I've only ever wanted you."

Dane ducks his head and tips my chin up with the rough pad of his thumb so our eyes lock. The sincerity in those gray orbs is almost blinding. I don't have to search his expression to know the truth.

One of his hands slips behind me and settles on my lower back. Dane bows his head and his bearded mouth glides over my neck and then the hollow of my throat, and my own head tips back as heat radiates through my body. He burrows his hand underneath the back of my sweater, fingertips playing over my spine like it's an instrument. And the music they elicit from me is a deafening cacophony of desire and need.

We sway together in small steps, my body tingling everywhere his touch lands. I throw my arms around his neck and draw him closer. My fingers tangle in the soft hair at his nape as his fingers dip lower and curl into my waistband.

He continues to pepper soft kisses along my collarbone and then both of his hands meet at the button of my jeans.

With a pop and a slide of my pants, a finger seductively glides back and forth like a pendulum, the tempo maddeningly slow.

His breath fans out over my neck and his voice in my ear is a low, strangled sound. "I want to feel how wet you are for me, Cherry." He toys with the edge of my panties, which elicits a loud gasp from me. "I want to make you come."

I'm not sure if this is an ask or a demand, but I'm all in. I hum in agreement.

With deliberate ease, he slips a finger underneath the silky material and straight through my wet folds. My entire body shivers involuntarily, my shuttering breath almost laughable.

Dane's fingers go straight to my core and into my soaked flesh. He spreads me open and sinks a digit inside. I clamp my hands over his shoulders to find purchase as I spasm around him.

"Ah, fuck, Cherry."

Without releasing his hand from its invasion between my legs, he spins me around so my back is flush to his chest. The hard ridge of his erection presses into the crease of my ass as his thumb works magic over my sensitive nub, expertly coaxing it toward the edge of euphoria with every swirl and tap.

With one hand down my pants, Dane tunnels the other under my sweater, cupping my breast and flicking my hardened nipple. I cry out from the rush of sensation that skitters through me like lightning striking. It's electric and powerful and if Dane didn't have me in his hold, I'd absolutely collapse to the floor in a heap.

I whimper out a small curse as he circles one nipple and then the other, all while his other thumb plays my clit like a harp. He strokes and caresses, flicks and massages, until I'm wound so tightly, I know I'll unravel before we reach the second chorus of the song.

He plunges a second finger deep, moving both in and out through my wet heat. I'm breathless and dizzy, already seeing stars emerging from the back of my eyelids. Pinpricks of pleasure scatter wildly as I reach the top of that precipice. Then I swan-dive off that cliff into the euphoric nirvana.

As if it's written in the stars that shine in the night sky. I am, without a single doubt, falling hard again for Dane.

And there is no stopping it this time.

33

———

Dane

With a week on the road playing three different teams on the East Coast of the US, it's been a challenge finding time to talk to Halle in real time. We've mostly resorted to text and Snapchat, and have only been able to get one video call in so far.

It's not enough.

Halle is like a drug to me. She consumes my thoughts in a way no one else ever has.

After our date, which ended soon after I made Halle come, we picked Lenni up from the Lundrens' house. Since it was late and Lenni was asleep in seconds after we got her into the car, I quietly carried my sleeping daughter into the house and put her to bed.

Something in my heart splintered open that night, like a stick splitting and breaking out on the ice after a hard connecting hit.

This little girl and her mom have changed me. I am not the same man I was before they came into my life.

Although there's still a twinge of resentment associated with how it all went down, Halle made the right call at the time by not telling me she was pregnant. I wasn't mature enough back then and I would've fled the responsibility, no matter what I tell myself now.

I wouldn't have wanted to take on the responsibility at that age and likely would have been an absent father, only sending child support and a birthday card every year.

I want to believe I would've done the right thing. I was raised by good parents and had strong familial support throughout my childhood, even when I lived apart from them during juniors. I know the indelible mark of a good father, because I had one.

So does Halle. And that means I understand her hesitancy to not let me get too close to Lenni. A pro hockey player's life is not the most stable. But my hope is that with each moment I spend with them, she cracks the door just a little further until someday soon, it'll allow me to step in and be Lenni's dad for life.

I'm back at the hotel in Cleveland tonight after a piss-poor game that we lost one to five. It was embarrassing and the team left the ice defeated and grumpy.

Of course, Rossco still argued we should go out to the clubs to erase our sorrows with booze and women. It took me fifteen minutes and a dozen excuses to get him off my back. He and Brewer, Wolf and the rookies—who I think might still be underage in the US—went to the bars without me.

So now I sit alone in a semidark room, stretched out on the bed with my phone in my hand, hoping Halle is available to chat.

> Me: Hey, Cherry. How was your day?

While I wait for her reply, ESPN recaps in the background all the highlights and lowlight moments of the games tonight. There's a clip of the horrible off-the-stick shot I made that wasn't even close to hitting anywhere in the net.

The phone in my hand vibrates, and a smile overtakes my face.

> Cherry: It was a day, for sure. But we watched the game. Lenni rooted for you. She did the Ax dance and cheered for her friend Ax.

My chest constricts. I'm literally still in the friend zone.

> Me: And how about you? Did you cheer for me?

> Cherry: Maybe...

She adds a wink emoji with a tongue sticking out. I chuckle.

> Me: Oh, come on, Cherry. You know you were glued to the TV while I played.

> Me: You were probably staring at my butt.

> Me: Or more likely, my stick. I know you like my stick.

Knowing her the way I do, I'd bet a million bucks she's blushing right now and hates it. In fact, I'm going to collect on that bet. I bring up her contact information and click the video chat button.

The screen displays my face first as it rings several times, then Halle's beautiful smile takes over the phone. And all is right with the world.

"Hey, you," I say, offering her a cheeky grin. "I was right."

Her brow wrinkles and those cute little groove lines pop out between them.

"That's unusual... you're not usually right." She snickers, and I give her playful glare. "Okay, what do you think you were right about?"

"You're blushing. And you're also obsessed with me."

She sputters with indignation, but there's no fire behind it. "I am not, you arrogant hockey boy!"

Turning on my side, I prop my head up on my bent arm; the other holds the phone and her image in my grasp.

She looks relaxed and comfortable in an old pink

robe, her hair up in a messy bun on the top of her head, her complexion shining with a radiant glow.

"So you were just hot and bothered with thoughts about me?"

Again, she snorts, but I see the change in her expression. She raises a hand to tuck back some hair behind her ear and bites on her lip as something flashes in her eyes.

"Did you just take a shower?"

"No, a bath. Why?"

My cock grows hard with the image of her slick, naked body in a bathtub. I reach down and adjust my shorts.

"Your face has a glow. And you look very comfortable." I lift a brow. "I bet you smell amazing, too."

She ducks her head down and sniffs. I bust out a laugh. "Well?"

Halle gives me a coy smile. "Vanilla and spiced orange. It's my fall go-to bath bomb."

My voice grows low and deep. "I wish it had been my mouth on you the other night, so I could've tasted you."

"Dane," she whispers breathlessly. Her eyes dart to something offscreen and moves off her bed. I can't see what she's going, but I can hear the lock clicking on her door. "If this is going where I think it's going, I don't want Lenni overhearing anything."

"Oh? Exactly where do you think it's going?"

My dick twitches, also intrigued as to the direction things might go from here.

Halle sits back down on the bed, switching off her

light so it's dark in her room, only a small light from her window casting a glow.

"Well…" She chews on her full bottom lip as I stare, licking my own lips. "I was hoping you'd get dirty with me."

I groan and palm the now hard bulge between my legs. I've imagined doing many sexual things with Halle, but phone sex never occurred to me. But I have no qualms about it. Whatever she wants, she's going to get, even if there's a chance we might get interrupted.

"Tell me, Cherry. What's on your dirty agenda?"

She clears her throat, and I can see the rise and fall of her chest. The V of her robe parts just enough that the enticing swell of her tits is visible.

"I feel bad there wasn't time to make you come the other night, too." Her eyes flash hot desire that lights a fire inside me, lust burning in my veins.

"And you want to do something about it now?"

"Mm-hmm," she murmurs. "I want to watch you. Touch yourself."

My lips curve into a sly grin. "Do you now, eh? You're turning into a bad girl for me, aren't you, Cherry?"

I slip my hand down the front of my shorts and wrap my fist around my straining cock.

Halle's cheeks turn a bright pink. "I'm…"

"Don't go shy on me now. I like seeing this side of you. It gets me so hard." I stroke my cock slowly, tight in my grip. My groan is deep and vibrates in my chest. I close my eyes momentarily and my head falls back into my pillow. Holding the phone above me, I lift my lids to stare at her.

Halle's gaze reflects my lust back to me.

"My cock is so hard for you right now. Open your robe and show me how you touch yourself too."

She hesitates only for a moment, her eyes flashing with uncertainty, but I can see a change almost immediately. Her indecision disappears and, in its wake, the look in her eyes offers a dare. It's a gorgeous feature on her.

Halle grasps the folds of her robe, pulling them apart to expose the supple swell that I dream of touching every night, then angles the phone so I see her breasts. The pertness of the round globes and the stiff peaks of her nipples have my abs clenching with anticipation.

"Go ahead," I encourage, voice raspy. "Play with your tits, baby."

She lets out a soft whimper as I watch her palm her fleshy mounds and rub her thumb over her hard nipples. She circles each turgid peak, which forces her back to arch off the bed. I watch, completely aroused and entranced by her seductive performance.

My own hand jerks faster now, gaining momentum with each erotic visual on display. Every breath and sound she makes drives me closer to eruption.

"Baby, I'm getting close. I want to watch you come, too." I struggle to form words as my fist jerks over the crown of my leaking cock. "Spread your legs and slide your fingers into that sweet pussy of yours."

Halle moans, and the sound is almost my undoing. "That's it, baby."

She pants breathlessly. Rapidly. The phone in her hand wobbles, shaking the image on my screen. But I don't care. It's such a beautiful sight to see her come undone like this. I only wish I was right there beside her doing it to her.

"Are you dripping wet, Cherry? Are you imagining it's my tongue licking and lapping at your pussy?"

"*Yeesss...*" she says, closing her eyes and raising her head off the pillow. "Dane... oh God. I'm there..."

With two more hard strokes, I growl out an orgasm and release all over my stomach. As I come down from that high, Halle's face returns to view. She's cloaked in darkness but for the strands of light pouring in from the streetlight, and she smiles softly.

"I've never done that," she admits quietly, eyelashes fluttering.

I wrinkle my nose. "Never? With anyone?"

She shakes her head. "You're the only one, Dane."

Something niggles in the back of my memory. She's said those words before, and I hadn't known what they meant.

A brilliant feeling explodes in my solar plexus. It's a goddamn gift to know I'm the only one she's chosen to do this with. A man she trusts enough to let go like that.

I want to be not just her first, or her last, but the only man from here on out.

We may not be perfect—I certainly have room to grow—but we can be a perfect match for each other.

34

____

Halle
   "Is Ax gonna come soon to help us make cookies, Mama?"

My heart does a little flip when Lenni uses Dane's nickname. She stares up at me with eyes that are so strikingly similar to Danes.

We're in the kitchen prepping for our cookie-making extravaganza for Lennon's birthday this week. I began this tradition last year when Lenni was old enough to help me with certain tasks in the kitchen. She stands on her pink polka-dotted step stool in an adorable kid-sized apron, her hair pulled back into a ponytail, and helps me roll out the dough we use to make her special cookies.

Next week, my baby turns five. She'll start kindergarten next fall, and in the blink of an eye, she'll be in high school, attending high school dances and getting her driver's license. The corners of my eyes fill with tears, and I blink them away, trying to focus on the present and not what the future holds.

I fold the sugar cookie dough a few more times and then hand it over to Lenni so she can flatten it out with her rolling pin.

"Yep, Dane should be here any minute. I invited him over just like you asked."

It was a few nights ago, when I was trying to get my ball of energy and chitty-chatty daughter to sleep, that she brought up Dane again. Her conversation style at bedtime is extremely meandery, even more so than during daylight hours, and it hits on several topics within a three-minute period. One of them this time was Dane.

"Mama, I don't like bedtime," she'd announced matter-of-factly.

I'd swept her hair from her face as she lay on her side, curled up with a pink bunny snuggled in her arms.

"Why's that, baby?"

"Because I don't like to close my eyes and fall asleep."

I gave her a smile. "But sleep is good for you. We all need our rest because that's when our bodies grow."

A cute frown marred her heart-shaped mouth. "But when I sleep, I can't play wiff Ax when he comes over to visit."

Son of a biscuit.

My heart had dropped to my stomach. Had she heard Dane and me fooling around when he stopped over the other night after his game? We've tried being so careful to be quiet. We don't need the inevitable questions that will arise if she wakes up to find Dane and me in an uncompromising position.

I quickly went with a diversion tactic instead of pretending Ax hadn't been by.

Smoothing her hair down, I bent over and placed a kiss on her forehead.

"Well, how about we invite him over for our cookie-making extravaganza this weekend? I think he's playing a home game Saturday night."

With an appeased grin, she had closed her eyes. I bent down to give her another hug and kiss then walked toward the door.

"I love you, sweet pea," I said from the doorway of her room. "Forever and always."

Lenni smiled dreamily. "Fowever and always."

You can only imagine the excitement Lenni has for today's event. The moment she woke up, it was nonstop Ax this and Ax that. It's highly amusing and very entertaining, but I think my kid might be a little obsessed with Dane.

Her mama might be too.

Speak of the devil.

My Ring doorbell notifies us of Dane's arrival and Lenni, covered in flour, jumps from her stool and rushes to the front door.

"Hang on, sweetie," I call out, grabbing a towel from the countertop and rushing after her. "We need to clean you off so you don't get Dane all mess—"

Towel in hand, I bend forward to wipe her off as she

swings open the door, and there's Dane standing at the threshold, dressed in snug jeans and a gray T-shirt the color of his eyes. I twist at my waist to stare at him. He looks like a snack.

"Hello, pretty ladies," he says with that boyish charm of his, amusement in his voice. "Don't you both look adorable in your matching aprons."

I straighten up and smile, gesturing with my arms out to the side. "It's our official cookie-making attire."

Dane steps inside and sweeps Lenni off her feet, swooping her over his head and flying her around. Lenni giggles and laughs with abandon, and my heart expands to ten sizes bigger inside my chest. It's such a sweet and tender reunion.

Under different circumstances, I could envision Dane coming home and Lenni squealing "Daddy" in delight.

I shake the mental picture from my mind and gesture toward the kitchen. "Lenni, let's show Dane what he's going to do."

"Okay, Mama."

Dane sets Lenni down on her feet, and she grabs hold of his hand and drags him into the kitchen amid nonstop chatter. Our gazes tangle in an exchange that sends tingly shivers down my spine. It's endearing and heartwarming, and I'm not at all sure I'll survive this if things with Dane change.

It's the reason I've delayed telling Lenni that Dane is her dad. She'd lose all of this if he disappeared and didn't make time to see her again. But maybe it wouldn't hurt as much if he's just her friend Ax.

Taking notice of her stool, Dane pretends to step up. "Oh, is this stool for me?"

Lenni scoffs, giving him a tiny shove on his leg. "Noooo, Ax! This is for me. I'm little. You're big."

He scuttles back, his arms flailing wildly in all directions.

Then she demonstrates by climbing up to stand on the step and lifting her arms out wide. "See? Now *I'm* big."

Dane tickles her ribs, and she squirms, expelling belly laughs that ring cheerfully around us. When I see the joy in both of their expressions, I look away, my heart squeezing tightly. I focus my gaze down to the dough and avoid the complexity of emotion that this scene conjures up for me.

"Okay you two. Enough goofing around," I say sternly, eyeing them both. "We have cookies to bake."

Dane sidles up between Lenni and me, his shoulder brushing against mine, and surveys the countertop covered in bowls and cookie sheets.

Standing beside me, he tilts sideways and puts his lips to my ear. "It smells so sweet in here. Is that you or the sugar?"

Goose bumps skitter down my arms, and my body vibrates so hard it's like he's shaking me like a ragdoll.

Dane's palms smack the countertop. "Okay, boss ladies. Put me to work. What should I do?"

I lean forward to peer around Dane at my daughter. "Lenni, why don't you have Dane roll out the dough and you pick out the cookie cutters to use?"

"Okay, Mama," she agrees obediently. She grabs the Tupperware box filled with a variety of cutters that had belonged to my mom before she passed away.

A pang of grief stabs me squarely in my chest. I remember doing this very same thing with my mom when I was a kid. My brothers were never interested in baking holiday cookies, so the activity belonged solely to me and Mom. Those are the moments I've cherished since she died and the same kind I want to pass on to Lennon.

While Lenni searches through the assortment, Dane's hand moves ever so discreetly behind my back. My spine tingles as his fingertips begin a maddening descent over my ass, landing squarely over my butt. Then he squeezes in what can only be defined as a precursor to what comes later after Lenni is in bed.

I chew my bottom lip and try to keep my heart from racing too wildly.

Checking the clock on the oven, I do the math and calculate the time for the cookies and when Lenni might go down for a nap. And when she does, I consider what might happen to fill that time.

I may end up eating something more than cookies.

The dirty thought gives me a secret thrill, and I covertly drop my own hand, slipping it between Dane and the cabinet, and cup his crotch.

A bear-like growl escapes his mouth, and I grin, drawing my hand back to the counter to accept a unicorn cookie cutter from Lenni, who dutifully doles one to each of us.

"Let's get baking," Dane says, tossing his up in the air and catching it in his palm. "I love to eat sweet things."

Tongue in cheek, he glances at me with a naughty quirk of his brow.

I draw a generous circle around my lips with my tongue. "Me too."

Dane gives me a saucy look and mouths, *It's on*.

35

D ane

Who knew baking cookies with a little girl would turn me into such a mush? Or that both she and her mom would steal my heart so completely?

Making cookies with Halle and Lennon today has made it the best day of my life. Possibly even surpassing the day I got drafted.

I enjoyed every minute of fun we had in the kitchen messing around and teasing Lenni—who is very opinionated and sassy—and even more so, flirting with Halle in very adult-content ways that flew right over Lenni's innocent head.

We made so many cookies that the kitchen table looked like a volcano erupted pink-frosted unicorn bodies all over it. Both Lenni and I somehow had colored icing smeared everywhere. It was in my beard, on the front of my shirt, even speckled over my jeans.

Which is why, after we gave Lenni a bath and put her to bed, I took a shower and Halle offered to wash my clothes.

Left with nothing else to wear while the clothes were in the laundry, I swing a towel over my hips and tuck it in at my navel before walking back to the kitchen to find Halle at the sink, still cleaning things up, her back to me.

Her back to me, I step in close and slip my hands around her middle. She jolts and then relaxes into me.

"Sorry, didn't mean to scare you." I place my lips at the base of her neck and run my nose up the vertebrae to her hairline, where wisps of hair have come loose from the knot at the top of her head. "But I've been dying to touch you."

Halle sighs, moving the baking pan to the drying rack next to the sink and then grasping the edge of the counter. She tips her head back to rest on my shoulder as I drag my lips along a span of skin. My tongue traces the shell of her ear and then licks over her jawline. She tastes and smells like sugar.

"Mm, that feels so good."

I continue to explore her flesh, one hand deftly untying the belted apron and pushing my hand underneath to palm her tits, as I murmur against her neck.

"Let me make you feel even better," I say in a low, hushed tone.

My hands moving to her hips, I spin her around to

face me as I tower over her. She gazes up at me with raw emotion. I feel it too. I close the gap between us and crush my lips against hers.

The kiss is deep, filled with longing and need, and transports me back to where we started.

Halle raises her hands to cover my biceps, her fingertips lightly stroking my arms, before wrapping her fingers around the muscles and clinging to me. The kiss takes on a frantic quality, tongues seeking one another in a tangled duel of desire.

She breaks the connection, her breath hitching rapidly as her eyes travel down my bare chest and then lower to the towel knotted below my navel.

"You're wearing a towel. In my kitchen."

A laugh busts out of my gut, and her eyes flash in alarm. I slam a hand over my mouth with a comical wide-eyed expression.

"Oh dear. You mean I'm naked under this cotton towel?"

I drop my hand and grasp her wrist, covering my heart with her palm. I slowly move her hand around my collarbone, over my pecs, and to my straining abs. I stop at the knot in the towel as our gazes connect. She quirks a brow in a dare.

And I gladly accept that challenge.

I drag her hand over the rock-hard cock that bulges from under the cotton towel. We both suck in a breath at the same time.

A corner of my mouth lifts into a sinful smirk. "If you

don't want me in a towel in your kitchen, maybe you'd prefer me naked in your bedroom."

Her eyes search mine—for what, I don't know—but she finally tugs my hand, pulling me behind her toward the bedroom.

I follow willingly but quietly so as not to wake our sleeping princess.

When we reach the bedroom, it's illuminated by a single light in the corner on the bedside table where a small white monitor sits, blinking a flashing green light.

Halle closes the door, locks it behind her, and raises a chin toward the device.

"It's a one-way monitor so I can hear if she calls out or wakes up."

I stalk toward her, dropping my towel as I do. When I stand in front of her, I frame her face with my hands and draw her in for a kiss. "So, we're free to fuck as loudly as we want and she won't hear us?"

She grins and covers my lips with a finger. "We still need to be quiet. We don't want any interruptions."

"I can be quiet as a church mouse," I whisper, then wink. "And as fast or slow as you want. I don't know about you, though. You like to make some noise."

She smacks me teasingly against my chest, but then I drop to the floor, the towel bunched beneath my knees. I undo her jeans and slide them down her legs, running my fingertips along the inside of her thighs as I do.

She steps out and kicks them away, leaving her standing in front of me in just her panties and T-shirt. I toy with the elastic edge at her stomach, slipping a finger underneath and gliding it over her mound.

She moans. *Loudly*.

I tip my head up to her, catching her eyes, and I give her a scolding tut. "Shh."

Halle gives me a playful whack on the side of my head, and I chuckle, but it's muffled because my mouth is now between her legs. I drag my nose, and then the tip of my tongue, around the material, breathing her in.

Unable to resist any longer, I yank her panties down and off her legs.

"Spread them for me, baby."

I wrap my fingers around the flesh of her thighs, thumbs gliding over the heat of her skin, and she widens her stance.

Her pussy is nice and trim and glistening with wetness. I lean in and take my first taste of Halle. My first taste in five years.

Fuck yeah. Halle tastes like sunshine, sugar, and some secret ingredient that's all hers.

My abs tighten and my cock twitches from her heady flavor. My tongue dives inside the seam of her folds, flickering over the sensitive bundle of nerves. Halle latches onto my hair and her nails bite into my scalp.

I do it again, swirling my tongue, but this time I add my thumb, tapping her swollen flesh in a tantalizing pattern that extracts a husky groan from Halle.

"That's right, baby. Ride me. Use me. Fuck my face."

Halle's hips begin to move in earnest, grinding against my mouth in search of her oblivion.

Her legs begin to tremble and shake, her fingers tightening in my hair to seek purchase while I continue to draw out more of her pleasure with my mouth.

Finally, her body stiffens. I push two fingers inside her dripping pussy and suck on her clit as she lets out a desperate and delicious keening sound. When I look up, she has her head thrown back and her mouth open as her legs tremble from her release.

"You okay, Cherry?" I ask, pulling away and swiping the back of my hand over my mouth. I sit back on my heels and take stock of her appearance.

It gives me so much pleasure to witness the smile that alights her face right now, to know I gave it to her.

I stand and reach for her, wrapping an arm around her waist and dragging her close. My hard cock strains against the wet heat of her entrance.

She sags against me, then tilts her head back to look at me. "Wow. That was just... wow."

I grin and waggle my brows. "If you think that's good, wait 'til you see what I can do with my cock."

Then I lift her off her feet and throw her on the bed, where she lands with a soft thud. The mattress dips when the weight of my knee presses into the mattress and crawl over her, tugging at the hem of her shirt to pull it off. Halle struggles, her arms getting stuck in the material, then wiggles free and tosses the shirt to the floor.

I straddle her legs and slip my hands behind her back

to undo the clasp of her bra, slowly dragging the straps down each arm. When she's completely bare, she lies back, and I take her all in.

The changes in her body are subtle. The swell of her breasts. The flare of her hips. The rise of her stomach. I touch her everywhere all at once, greedy to worship her with everything I've got now that we're here. If I could, I'd spend all night showing her how gorgeous she is to me. But I know that, with Lenni asleep across the hallway, our time together could be cut short. So I make what little time we have together count.

I'm at a loss for words to describe how beautiful she is with her auburn hair all mussed and fanning out over the mattress. Her cheeks are still rosy from her orgasm, and her eyes are a muted blue, like a sunrise sky.

I bend down and suck a nipple between my lips, swirling my tongue over its stiff peak. Halle squirms underneath me, mewling softly, her back arching up off the bed. The move pushes more of her breast into my mouth, and I palm the other, flicking the pad of my thumb over the nipple.

I slowly inch my way down her body, placing kisses along her dewy skin, trailing my tongue down her sternum. With my head at her stomach, I roll my tongue around her navel and run my hand over the curve of her hip.

Shifting to my side, I press my fingers into the flesh of her inner thigh, prying it open and slipping my fingers inside her heat.

"Oh, God," she cries out softly when I curl two fingers and slide them in and out. Then her hand darts out, reaching down to wrap her fingers around my wrist. "Dane. Please. I need you inside me."

My eyes fly to hers. "You sure?"

She smiles, spreading her legs to accommodate my body and pulls me back on top of her. As I settle my hips over her pelvis, aligning my cockhead at her entrance, I tentatively rock my hips forward. The heat from her slick center has me hissing out an expletive.

Before we reignited this sexual exploration again with each other, we had a conversation about our sexual health and birth control methods. Obviously, having learned the lesson the hard way, we know exactly what can happen if not careful.

But this time, Halle is on an almost foolproof contraceptive method, and I confirmed I received a clean bill of health from my most recent physical. It's always good practice to have regular checkups, anyhow.

It gave us both peace of mind that I could go ahead without the need for anything between us.

"I'm sure. Are you?" I can hear the smile in her voice, and I reach down and nip at her earlobe.

"I've never been surer in my life."

36

———

Halle

"Ahh, fuck, Cherry. You're perfect," Dane says reverently, positioning his cock at my entrance and then guiding himself inside. It takes me a bit to adjust to his size, and I wince inaudibly as my walls stretch and tighten around him. "Are you okay? Need me to stop?"

You'd think that never having another lover outside of Dane years ago would make me a bit rusty and uncoordinated, but as they say, it's just like riding a bike. And honestly, Dane does most of the work with his athletic physique and prowess.

I reach up and bite his lower lip, tugging on it before letting go.

"Keep going. I'm good."

He's so commanding yet gentle that it brings tears to the edges of my eyes. The confidence he instills in me and the appreciation he demonstrates for my body is a reminder that I am a sexy woman. A wanted woman. Not just a mom, sister, or daughter.

I am his for the taking.

It's the first time I've felt him inside me without a condom, and it is unreal.

I trail my fingernails down the column of his spine, scouring over the contours of taut muscles that flex and lead to his fabulous butt.

It's so true what they say. Dane is proof that hockey butts are the best.

He thrusts inside me, my walls gripping his steely cock in a tight vice, and I draw my knees up to bring him deeper. A sexy growl of appreciation vibrates from his chest.

"It feels so good to be inside you again, Cherry," he murmurs into my ear, his breath fanning through my hair. He picks up his pace, hips driving forward and back, and holds nothing back.

Our eyes lock, intensity electrifying between us. He hovers over me, and the momentum slows. Then his hips stop rocking when he thrusts inside to the hilt, hitting me deep in my core.

"That night when you touched yourself for me... fuck, baby. It was the hottest thing I've ever seen." He reaches behind and snags my wrist, raising it above my head. "But tonight, that honor is all mine."

He slips the other hand between us and finds my needy clit, circling it with practiced measure.

I buck into him, seeking the pleasure out, and he huffs out a heady breath.

"I want you to come again, baby. I want you to see stars and scream my name."

Dane draws his thumb in tight strokes over my sensitive clit, and a tidal wave of pleasure builds deep in my core. He continues to undulate his hips, faster and harder, lodging inside me so deep I do see stars.

I slip my fingers through his and squeeze his hand hard as my climax crests, sending wave after glorious wave slamming through me.

I'm completely oblivious to how loud I am when I cry out in pleasure. But in this blissed-out state, I can scarcely consider the consequences.

A slow, sexy smirk spreads across his full lips, and his heavy eyes regard me with something I can't name.

He dips his head and fits his mouth over mine, kissing me deeply before rearing back. His eyes close, and he pants out choppy breaths. I swing my legs around his waist, hooking my ankles against his lower back to facilitate a closer connection as his bulk and weight press against me.

And oh, my word. It feels so good that a husky sound I don't even recognize shudders up from my chest.

"Fuck, Cherry." He makes a strangled noise, and I feel his body tighten when he erupts, pulsing his release inside me.

Contentment steals over me while he rolls off me and

onto his back, fitting me underneath his outstretched arm.

Something awakens inside me as I curl into his chest, burying myself in his warmth and masculine scent. My heart lurches and I bask in the sensation of being held.

I tilt my head up to peer at Dane, who breathes in deep and even breaths, his eyes closed, a look of contentment on his face.

"You're staring."

I jerk away and bury my face into his side. He chuckles but lifts my chin with his thumb and finger, so our eyes meet again.

The question has been stirring inside my head since something he said earlier. It's a humiliating need to know, even though I'm scared of the truth.

"Can I ask you something?"

Dane runs a hand over the top of my head, brushing the wild hair from my eyes. Amusement bubbles in his tone.

"If the question is whether we can go again right now, the answer is, give me five minutes to rebound."

"I'm being serious here," I grouse, pinching his side—which is difficult to do because the skin is so hard over his ribs. But I get my point across with it anyhow.

Then I run my finger along the smooth center of his torso, stopping at his navel, circling it, and returning the journey back to his pecs.

"Is the sex you've had with other"—I swallow and feel

a blush rise over my face—"women the same? I mean, does it feel the same way?"

He pins me with a wicked and teasing grin. "Is it like this with the other men you've been with, Cherry?"

The bitter truth gets lodged in the back of my throat, and I cough.

Do I come clean and tell the honest but embarrassing truth about my nonexistent sex life? Or laugh it off like this is totally chill and just another day in the life of me.

"Well?" he prods, shifting to his side to face me, both our heads sharing the pillow, noses and mouths inches apart.

His fingers gently feather over my collarbone, my shoulder, and then down the slope of my arm, leaving goose bumps in their wake. This intimacy is so nice. We rarely, if ever, had this opportunity in the past, moments where we could enjoy each other's company post-coital. We were usually in a car or a location where we could've been discovered.

I suppose the same applies now, but in this case, it wouldn't be my dad or brothers who would barge in. It would be a sweet little girl who would ask a whole lot of questions about why her friend Ax is naked in my bed.

The blush deepens. Dane brushes hair from my face and tucks it behind my ear.

Okay, here goes nothing.

"I don't have any other experience to compare it to. You've been the only one."

His head rears back and his nose scrunches. "Seriously?"

"Yes." I push my face into the pillow and cover my head with my hand.

"Hey, don't do that." He places his hands on my shoulders and rolls me back over, prying my thighs open with his knee to position said erection between my legs. "I think it's fucking hot, and makes me hard knowing it."

He lowers his lips to mine and kisses me deeply and thoroughly. "What's embarrassing to me is that I went through one after another, trying to find something I couldn't."

I peer up at him with wide eyes. "What was that?"

Dane skims my cheek with his thumb and then rolls it over my lips. I shiver at the touch.

"I was always looking for you."

"THAT'S ALL IT TOOK?" Carmy chokes out in disbelief, squawking at the pitch a prepubescent boy's voice. "Cookies?"

I cover my mouth to stifle the giggle.

"He had you at his mad baking skills?"

I adjust my position in bed and pull the sheet up to my chin, allowing the thoughts of the sex I had with Dane to drift back through my head.

I had wanted to talk privately with Carm, so I called her early this morning before Lenni woke up. I was bursting at the seams to share all the sexy bits and details about my night with Dane.

And heavenly biscuits, what a night it was.

I clench my thighs together to rid myself of the ache that remains from the aftereffects of last night. From the delicious and dirty fucking Dane gave me.

This wasn't the eighteen-year-old horny hockey boy I once knew. This was a man who'd grown and matured. Who had gained patience and endurance and learned some impressive techniques and tricks along the way.

I sigh. "It was more than the fact that he spent the day baking with us, Carm. Not only was he so sweet with Lenni, but oh my God, what he did to my body. I completely forgot I was someone's mother and let that man do things to me that make me blush. He should receive an award for giving orgasms."

"Oh, yeah?" She tips her head, a sassy gleam in her eye. "How many, Hal?"

"I lost count after three."

She whistles. "Damn, girl. He's come a long way since your first time."

"Trust me, he's as good with his stick in bed as he is out on the ice."

"Atta girl. It's about time you get to experience the amazing sex you deserve."

We chat for a little while longer until Carmen says she needs to get ready to go to a study group, then make plans to talk later in the week. I'd asked her to come for Lenni's birthday party, but she's unable to get away right now, but promises to come visit over the holidays.

I roll to my side and set the phone back on the cradle, hoping Lenni will sleep in today so I can relax a while longer. Truth is, I need the rest because I did not sleep a wink in this bed with Dane.

The way he touched me left me breathless and restless for surrender of my body. He explored my breasts. My face. My stomach. My pussy. My entire body is craving its next hit of the Ax. I chuckle at my own humor and begin to doze off as I remember last night in bed with Dane.

37

————

D^{ane}

Today is Lennon's fifth birthday.

My daughter—who I just learned existed not even a month ago—is turning five.

The same daughter who still has no idea I'm her dad and thinks of me only as "friend Ax." The girl whose relationship to me remains something no one else knows about. Not even my parents.

I've become increasingly frustrated and impatient over this fact, but I haven't pushed Halle to make the announcement. The longer we hold off, the more time that slips by where Lenni doesn't know me as her dad. Time that she could get to know her grandparents and her aunts—my sisters—who would absolutely jump into their roles with arms wide open.

But Halle has her reasons for not telling Lenni about

me, and no matter what I say to try and change her mind or resolve her fears, she keeps putting me off.

Her concerns are valid, but our perspectives different. I've done everything I can to build her trust in me and to show her she can count on me to be here for her and Lenni. Even if I have to move.

Because of my career, there's always a possibility that I might have to move and won't live near Lennon. But plenty of fathers—hockey players or not—deal with the problem of distance, and good ones make sure it doesn't impact their relationship with their kids.

I wish I could guarantee Halle that I will always remain in Vancouver. If my career lasts as long as I hope, though, there's a high probability that I will at some point not be a Viking. It's just the way things are. Even now, although I'm currently under a five-year limited-trade contract, I could be put on waivers or simply be traded to one of the few places I've agreed to, and my contract goes with me.

But I've promised Halle that if that happens, I will always make Lennon my number one priority. And Halle, too, for that matter. I would move heaven and earth to keep our connection strong.

And that's the truth. We've become almost insepa-rable these past few weeks and whenever I have free time —outside of practice, publicity, travel, and games—I spend it with them.

They've become my world.

And I've fallen—for a second time—for Halle. I just

can't seem to tell her this. I struggle with the words *I love you*. Up to this point, I've only told her I care deeply for her and Lennon. It's a dick move and I know it.

But I think today is the day.

After the party guests leave and Lenni is in bed, when Halle and I can have our alone time, I plan to tell her how I feel. Who knows, maybe that will change her outlook on sharing our secret with Lennon.

Happy with my decision, I park the car in the driveway and start unloading all the wrapped gifts I got for Lenni. I may have gone a little overboard, but your daughter only turns five once, and I want her to remember it for the rest of her life.

With a smile affixed to my face and a tower of boxes in my arms, I walk up the steps and knock against the door with a kick of my booted toe.

I can hear Lenni squealing inside, and my heart swells through my ribs. Jesus Christ, that little girl has stolen my heart in mere weeks.

Seems apropos for the MacAlister girls, considering Halle did the same when we first met.

The front door swings open and standing on the other side of the threshold are two of the most beautiful girls in the world.

Lenni dances and twirls on her toes in a pink tutu-like dress, complete with little pink flowers adorning the top. And standing next to her is, without a doubt, the girl of my dreams. A woman whose smile is brighter than the fucking sun and whose lips were made for kissing.

"Dane, what in the world did you do? Buy out the entire store?"

She shakes her head and steps aside as I make my way to the living room, where I hope to find a place to set down the presents.

"Hey Lulu Lennon," I greet, giving her a big, cheesy grin. "I hear it's someone's birthday today. I'm not sure whose, but maybe you can help me with these presents?"

I bend down as if to relinquish them to her and then pretend to lose my balance, juggling the gift boxes as if they might fall. My ruse works, and she howls in a fit of giggles.

She lifts her hands in the air and dances around. "It's my birfday, Ax! I'm five today."

Setting the boxes on the coffee table, I give her an incredulous expression, my mouth gaping open as I slap a hand over it.

"What? You're kidding me. I thought you were at least fifteen!"

Lenni stomps her foot and places her hands on her hips with sass. "Uh-uh. I'm *five!*" Then she lifts her palm and spreads her fingers, counting them off for me.

"Wow, you're very smart for a five-year-old. I'm very impressed. Give me a high five for that."

She reaches up on her tiptoes and slaps my hand with hers.

And with the curiosity of a kid on her birthday, she turns her attention to the gifts. She walks over and examines each one, then glances over her shoulder at me.

"Can I open them now, Ax?"

Knowing I'm not the authority figure when it comes to the timing for gift opening, I turn to grab Halle's attention, only to find that she's already watching us from the kitchen, wearing a look I've never seen before.

It's a combination of bittersweet melancholy and a deep, unshakable love.

"Hey, Mom? Can she open one of her presents?" I look at Lenni and encourage her hands clasped in a prayer to beg. "Pwetty please... ?"

Halle puts her own hands on her hips and tilts her head, closing one eye as if deliberating.

"Hmm... I don't know... maybe just one..."

My eardrums are pierced when Lenni screams in delight, drowning out Halle's next statement.

"And then you and Dane need to help put all the food on the table."

I kneel on the floor next to Lenni, wrapping an arm around her tiny waist, and shove my face close so I can whisper in her ear. "Which one do you want to start with?" I ask, watching her examine each one carefully, considering each before choosing the winning box.

"This one," she announces, picking up the box with a large pink bow.

When I'd asked Halle what I should consider getting Lenni, I already knew my daughter loved all things princess, so with Halle's approval, I bought her a vanity case filled with glitter makeup, princess crowns, plastic earrings, and even a set of sparkly shoes.

Lenni tears through the wrapping paper, gleefully exclaiming when she sees the gift hidden by it.

"Oh! I love it! Look, Mama." She holds up box to show Halle, who has wandered into the room and sits down on the edge of the sofa.

"Wow, that is so cool. What do you say to Ax?"

With the speed of a professional hockey player, Lenni spins around, throws her arms around my neck, and gives me the biggest, hardest hug of my life.

"Thank you, Ax. I love you."

I'm still floating on cloud nine from my daughter's declaration of love a few hours ago when Cale, Nils, and I step out in the backyard where a cooler of beer sits on the porch.

With the cramped living space inside and the number of birthday party attendees, including Halle's dad and one of her brothers, we decided we needed some breathing room after Lenni got a new bike from her Papa.

I'm not sure if Lenni was more excited about the present or to be reunited with her Uncle Drew and Papa.

The back patio has no furniture to accommodate the three of us, so we stand around and pop open our light and NA beers. Since tomorrow we start a travel week, we are following our usual rule of no drinking.

"Cute kid," Costa finally says with beer in hand, nodding his head toward the house before taking a swig.

He was a little stunned to have been invited to attend a kid's birthday party, but Halle was adamant that we invite Cale and Sommer over to celebrate since they had us over to their place.

Unfortunately, Costa came alone because Sommer wasn't feeling well enough to travel up here after her latest infusion earlier in the week. Costa's understandably worried and frustrated that he can't be with her, wherever it is she lives. I haven't outright asked, but I think she's in the US, somewhere on the West Coast.

The sounds of little-girl giggles coming from inside drifts out the door, and I glance back through the window to see Lennon and Elise being chased around the house by Drew. He's got his arms raised above his head, and he lumbers around pretending to be some kind of monster.

A smile forms at the corners of my mouth, and when I turn around, Cale gives me a strange look. I shrug, quickly washing down my secret with a swig of beer.

"What exactly is going on here, Ax? Are you playing house with Halle and her kid?"

My head snaps back at his judgment. "What? No. It's not like that."

Nils coughs, and I glare at him.

"It does seem oddly suspicious," Nils adds, rolling a thumb over the top of his beer bottle. "You do spend a lot of time with them for being just friends. Just saying."

"Not you, too, Lundy. Fuck you both." My words aren't

bitter, but I'm feeling protective and defensive about my relationship at the moment.

There are legitimate questions that under normal circumstances, I could answer easily. Except this is not whatever would be considered normal, and I can't tell them the entire truth. Halle isn't just any woman, and Lennon not only owns a piece of my heart but also shares my DNA.

Costa leans against the house and crosses an ankle over his foot.

"Maybe it's just my imagination, but Lennon sure looks a lot like you, Ax." He cocks his head. "Do my eyes deceive, or is she your kid?"

Oh, shit.

There it is.

The observation that leads to a question that I'm not supposed to answer.

But fuck me. These two are my good friends, and I know they won't gossip or tell anyone else on the team. If they promise not to say a word to anyone and the secret remains in our cone of silence, I don't see how it can hurt if I reveal the truth.

"Yeah, about that…" I take a deep breath and blow it out. "Halle and I kind of dated when we were teens. It was my last season in juniors before I was drafted."

"What does 'kind of dated' mean?" Lundy asks, that always skeptical brow of his lifting even further to the sky.

"It means, we didn't date for very long. But long enough for me to get her pregnant."

"Mm-hmm," Costa says, nodding as if it all makes perfect sense now. "So you broke up with her when she found out she was pregnant? That's a douchebag move."

"Fuck no. I never would have done that. We broke up, yeah, but at the time, we had no idea she was pregnant. I was in the dark all this time that we had a kid together. I never knew I was Lenni's dad until just recently."

There's a noise behind us, and we all swing around to see Lennon on the doorstep, a cookie in one hand, a new doll in the other, and a confused expression slashed across her face.

She blinks and then stares directly at me.

And then time slows down, and the world drops out from under my feet.

"You're not my daddy! I don't have a daddy!"

38

Halle

The party came to a quick conclusion and had cleared out quickly after Lenni had come running back into the kitchen with giant crocodile tears streaming down her sticky face, sobbing uncontrollably. Her words were such a jumbled mess that it took me two times to decipher what she was saying, but I knew it the moment I saw the look on Dane's face.

Lenni had already been emotionally and physically tired from the excitement of the party, sugary treats, and playtime she'd had with her new friends and my brother, which made it the perfect storm for this to happen. It was as explosive as if the mass of balloons in my living room had all popped at once.

I brought her into her room while Dane said goodbye to everyone and now I'm trying to get to the bottom of the story.

I kneel beside Lenni and wrap her sweaty body in my arms. "Baby, what's wrong? Why are you crying?"

She hiccups, and tears pour from her eyes. "Ax isn't my daddy. He said he's my daddy, but I don't have a daddy."

I rear back, confused why she would say such a thing. When I look at her sad expression, my heart breaks. I shouldn't have let this go on so long, and that regret lies squarely on me, and the burden of that shame on my shoulders alone.

A tall shadow materializes at the doorway, blocking out the overhead hallway light. I glance up to see a panic-stricken expression marring Dane's face.

What the hell happened? I mouth, my hands shaking violently with a simmering, protective anger I've never felt before.

He shakes his head and mouths back, *I'm so sorry*.

I stand then, scooping Lenni up in my arms, settling her on my lap on her bed, then, with a chin nod and glare, direct Dane to come in.

He stands rigid and back stiff, his jaw is tightly clenched. I glance at him for a second but then look away for fear my own tears will start to fall.

I know I brought this heartache on myself. My indecision around telling her about Dane since we've been in Vancouver, and then, apparently a slip that Lenni overheard have finally created the backlash I'd hoped to avoid altogether.

Lenni's tears have stopped flowing now, and she rests

her head against my arm. My daughter is so tired from today's event, and once again, the timing of this conversation couldn't be any worse.

But I can't avoid the truth any longer.

"Lenni, baby," I begin, placing my hand over her tiny palm. It's still sticky from the cookie frosting. "Dane and I need to talk to you about what you heard him say outside. Okay?"

She nods, lifting her head to peer through wet lashes at Dane. I give him a chin nod, and he takes a step toward us, bending down to kneel in front of the bed. His gray eyes search mine for direction. I'm not sure I have any for him, so I only offer a soft smile.

Dane takes hold of Lenni's other hand. "Hey Lulu Lennon. I'm so sorry you had to hear the truth that way."

Lenni cocks her head to look at Dane and then lifts her face up to mine. "Mama? Is Ax really my daddy?"

I can only nod and smile, tears flooding my eyes. The words get trapped in my throat like a boulder refusing to budge.

"Yeah, honey. Dane is your daddy."

She thinks about this for a second, wiggling with the uncontainable energy of a child.

"Is that why he kisses you?"

My eyes snap to Dane's, wide with shock. He quirks an eyebrow and the corners of his mouth rise into that boyish smirk of his. *Ugh.*

"What? Why do you say that?"

"'Cuz I saw him kiss you in the kitchen." She stops to

think about this for a moment, and then adds, "And on the couch. And on your bed."

My mouth gapes open. Dane chuckles, then bites down on his lip in an effort to contain the sound, and I want to kick him in the kneecap.

"When did you see that?"

She shrugs, but it's apparent that we haven't been as stealthy with our hookups as we thought we were. Lenni must've witnessed some of that over the course of the last few weeks.

Dane jumps in to save the conversation and keep me from dying of embarrassment.

He lifts Lenni's hand and places a kiss on top of her knuckles, his dark lashes framing his gray eyes, which have turned soft and light.

"Lenni, your mom and I like each other. A lot. In fact, I love her. That's why you saw us kissing." He glances at me with a tender expression. My eyes grow wide from his admission. But I set it aside for now as he continues. I watch the Adam's apple in his throat bob up and down as he swallows. "We liked each other a lot a long time ago, and that's why you were born."

I mean, it's not exactly the full birds and bees explanation, but at least it gets the point across to a five-year-old as to how she came into being. There is truth there.

"Do you understand what Dane means?" I ask, searching her face to see if she is grasping this explanation.

She nods but purses her lips in consideration. "But

how come I didn't know Ax" —hesitates for a moment and then floors me when she changes the name—"I mean Daddy, before? Why doesn't he *live* with us like Elise's daddy does?"

Oof. That's the million-dollar question.

Okay, I'm prepared for this. Aren't I? I've thought long and hard on how I'd answer this in a way a little girl could comprehend.

"It's complicated," Dane and I both say at the same time. We laugh, and it eases the tension as he gestures for me to continue.

"Baby, when you were growing in Mommy's tummy, Dane—your daddy—was far, far away. He didn't know I was pregnant with you. And he didn't know when you were born."

Lenni jumps in excitedly to add her take. "But Ax is here now and that's why he can be my daddy now?"

My eyes connect with Dane's, and I see a certainty and commitment reflecting back at me. I know unequivocally that this is the right thing to do.

He deserves the chance to be involved in his daughter's life, and Lenni deserves to have a dad who loves her, will protect her and be there for her as she grows, even when and if he doesn't live in the same city as she does.

My heart swells with love for the future these two will share together.

"I would love to be your daddy, Lulu Lennon," Dane says, wearing his heart on his sleeve as he stares at his little girl with tears in his own eyes. He extends his arms, and in a flash, Lenni jumps into his embrace, throwing her arms around his neck.

"Do you love me, Daddy?"

Dane lets out a booming laugh and falls backward onto the floor with Lenni on top of him. He tickles her ribs, and she squirms and giggles while my heart explodes with love for them both.

"I love you, my daughter," Dane whispers into her ear, hugging her to his chest. And then he pins me with his gaze. "And I love your mom too, very much."

"Fowever and always," his daughter replies, and I can't help it. The tears come hard and fast.

She pushes up from Dane's chest and stands, taking the two steps toward me. She reaches up on tiptoes to cup my face in her hands, and gives me the most earnest look I've ever seen.

"It's okay, Mama. I still love you too, fowever and always."

Forever and always.

EPILOGUE

Dane – 1 Year Later

"Daddy's home! Daddy's home!"

The sound of my little girl's voice as she runs down the hallway to greet me is the best sound in the world. Well, a close second might be the sound her mother makes when I make her come.

I set down the heavy gear bag on the hallway floor just in time to catch Lenni, clad in her little piggy-footed pjs, as she launches herself into my arms. She wraps her arms around my neck and squeezes me tight, smelling of bathtime and baby shampoo.

"You're up late, Lulu Lennon," I say against damp hair that has been set into a braid. Lifting my eyes over her head, I see Halle coming around the corner carrying a Vikings mascot plushie in her hand.

Halle exhales heavily and as she gets closer, I can see the dark circles under her eyes.

"Someone was being stubborn and would not go to bed until her daddy got home and tucked her in with a bedtime story."

I swing my gaze to Lenni, who smiles brightly, her chin cleft widening with her grin.

"Hmm. Good thing the team plane was on time so I could be here to read a story, then." I brush my nose over her smooth face, and she turns so we can give each other angel kisses. She giggles, and I set her back down on the ground.

"I want you to tell me the story about the ice hockey monster, Ivan Ruski. He's the mean one."

"But you know that story by heart now, sweetie. How about I tell you a new one?" I ask, meeting Halle's gaze and rolling my eyes.

When our girl likes or latches onto something, she is dead set on doing it on repeat. It's a compulsive trait she might have gotten from me.

The one thing I don't mind doing over and over again, however—besides hockey, of course—is Halle. Goddamn, things between us are as hot and good as ever.

The last year of my life has been a lesson in becoming a good dad and an even better partner. I've learned a lot, especially after we made the decision for Halle and Lennon to move in with me.

Now that's something that's made me grow up in a hurry. Becoming a dad to Lenni is so much fun, and every day is a new opportunity to witness how my little girl's brain operates. And Lord help me, but I've found out that being a girl dad is much like having a unicorn vomit pink all over your life.

But I wouldn't have it any other way.

Living together in my house has also made coming home after long, difficult road trips something of an adventure. Lenni will tell me about all the new information she learned during her days at school. My girl is in kindergarten now and loves everything about school. She'll display any new artwork she's made that will be hung on our fridge door, and she'll demonstrate all her new dance moves she makes up on the spot.

And once we put the little rascal to bed and ensure that she's fast asleep, I get to be a rascal in a very different way in the bedroom I now share with Halle.

Which is what I plan to do tonight.

Or, from the way she looks right now, maybe just a bath and a massage are what the doctor ordered.

"Hey, baby," I say, looping my arm behind her back and tucking her in for a hug. I place a kiss on her forehead and then bend to cover her mouth with mine. Her lips part seductively for me, and I sweep my tongue inside.

"Mm... I've missed you," she says, peering up at me in that sexy manner of hers. She licks her lips, and I know exactly what she's thinking as I slide my hands down her spine until I reach the curve of her ass, squeezing it suggestively.

"Are you looking for a naughty bedtime story of your own tonight?" I give her a wink, tangling my fingers with hers as we follow our daughter upstairs to her bedroom.

"I was thinking about taking a nice, *long,* hot bath."

I lift a brow. "Oh? That sounds...*hot.*"

"Oh, it will be," she promises, her eyes flashing with possibility.

With Lenni having already run into her bedroom, I halt my steps and spin Halle around, shoving her against the hallway wall.

I lean forward and press my growing erection into her core, undulating my hips in a wickedly sexy move. Reaching for her hands, I pin them above her head, then take her lips in a possessive kiss.

"Fuck, I missed you. And I am going to give you an R-rated version of story time as soon as I can."

Lenni prattles on in the distance as she sings a bedtime song to her stuffies while I kiss the hell out of her mother, bringing a hand between us and slipping my fingers down her panties.

I hiss out a not-so-G-rated expletive when I find her slick with need already.

"Fuck me, Cherry," I groan, tugging her lower lip between my teeth. "Go get that bath started. I'm about to tell the fastest bedtime story in the history of bedtime stories. And when I'm done, I want to find you wet and slick for me."

I slap her ass as she turns to walk into our bedroom. She looks back over her shoulder with a grin.

"Hurry up, baby." She blows me a kiss. "I love you."

"I love you, too, Cherry."

I watch the one woman I love more than anything in the world, who has changed me into the man I am today, close the door behind her.

Then I step into the room of the sweetest little girl in the world, who I love more than anything too, because she's made me her daddy.

And I think to myself, how lucky can one man get?

THE END

NEXT UP IN THE VANCOUVER VIKINGS SERIES

Want some more hockey romance from the Vikings?

Next up in the series is Wolf's book in *Off the Post*.

🐺 Grumpy/Sunshine ☀️

👨‍👧 Teammates younger sister

🐟 Fish Out of Water

💙 Loner/Emotional Scars

Soren "Wolf" Wolfenspiel is the hero between the pipes that can pounce on a puck like a wolf on its prey. Off the ice, though, he's a grumpy loner with a heart of stone who prefers to be left alone. Until he agrees to pose for his teammate's charity calendar and meets the woman who will change his life and a little boy who will melt away the ice in his heart.

COMING SOON - PREORDER NOW

ACKNOWLEDGMENTS

To the Fagan sisters: Debbie and DeeDee
Thank you for the crazy night we had at the dive bar in Vancouver when DeeDee shared the story about how her husband won you over. Debbie shouted out, "Nacho cheese? That's all it took?" I thought that was the funniest thing I'd ever heard and wrote it down so I could use it in my next book. You'll find a similar line in Chapter 36 during the conversation between Halle and Carmen. 😊

To former UW hockey player Daniel Smith
You were a godsend and a wealth of information for my research on hockey operations. Thanks for all the details of how hockey operations work. 🏒

And of course, to my editor, Sandy, 📝 who always gives me the feedback and perspective I need to enhance my storyline and character arcs to create a better book. You are my rock. Thank you for being so fabulous, encouraging, and a true hockey fan.

To my assistant, Melissa

You make it so easy for me to do my thing because I know everything will be handled on my behalf. If I don't say it enough, I appreciate you!

ABOUT THE AUTHOR

Sierra Hill is a *2020 RONE Award-Winning* author of *Game Changer*, as well as over 50 novels, including the award-winning college sports series, *Courting Love*, and the twice award-finalist erotic ménage serial, *Reckless – The Smoky Mountain Trio*.

Subscribe to her email list and download a FREE book here: www.sierrahillbooks.com

And don't forget to look for me on one of these socials:

ALSO BY SIERRA HILL

Vancouver Vikings Hockey

Offside (A Vancouver Vikings Series Book #1)

Off the Stick (A Vancouver Vikings Series Book #2)

Off the Post (A Vancouver Vikings Series - Book #3)

College Hockey

Playmaker (A World of True North Moo U novel)

The Hockey Player and the Tutor

The Puget Sound Pilots (Sports Romance)

The Girlfriend Game (Book #1)

The Wife Win (Book #2)

The Rival Romeo (Book #3)

Change of Hearts (A College Campus Series)

Game Changer (Book #1)

Change in Strategy (Book #2)

Change of Course (Book #3)

Courting Love (College Sports)

Full Court Press

The Rebound

Pivot

Fast Break

Jump Shot

College Football - *Clearview Falls University* series

Falling for the Fake Boyfriend Book 1

Falling for the Roommate Book 2

Falling for the Football Player Book 3

Falling for the Quarterback Book 4